"Noooo!"

Lily uttered a terrified moan as more of the hot red liquid sprayed over her face, dripped down the front of her T-shirt.

Where was it coming from? Where?

From the rolling press?

With mounting horror Lily wiped the blood from her face. Stepped closer to the printing press.

Whoa.

The press wasn't running as she had thought. The big paper wheel was jammed.

Jammed by . . . jammed by . . .

"NOOOOOO!" Lily's hoarse scream echoed through the vast plant.

The paper wheel was jammed by a head and shoulders.

Graham's head. Graham's shoulders.

"Graham—!" she choked out. "Are you alive? Are you still alive?"

Books by R. L. Stine

Fear Street

THE NEW GIRL
THE SURPRISE PARTY
THE OVERNIGHT
MISSING
THE WRONG NUMBER
THE SLEEPWALKER
HAUNTED
HALLOWEEN PARTY
THE STEPSISTER
SKI WEEKEND
THE FIRE GAME
LIGHTS OUT
THE SECRET BEDROOM
THE KNIFE
PROM QUEEN
FIRST DATE
THE BEST FRIEND
THE CHEATER
SUNBURN
THE NEW BOY
THE DARE
BAD DREAMS
DOUBLE DATE
THE THRILL CLUB
ONE EVIL SUMMER
THE MIND READER
THE WRONG NUMBER 2
TRUTH OR DARE
DEAD END
FINAL GRADE
SWITCHED

Fear Street Super Chiller

PARTY SUMMER
SILENT NIGHT
GOODNIGHT KISS
BROKEN HEARTS
SILENT NIGHT 2
THE DEAD LIFEGUARD
CHEERLEADERS: THE NEW EVIL

The Fear Street Saga

THE BETRAYAL
THE SECRET
THE BURNING

Fear Street Cheerleaders

THE FIRST EVIL
THE SECOND EVIL
THE THIRD EVIL

99 Fear Street: The House of Evil

THE FIRST HORROR
THE SECOND HORROR
THE THIRD HORROR

Other Novels

HOW I BROKE UP WITH ERNIE
PHONE CALLS
CURTAINS
BROKEN DATE

Available from ARCHWAY Paperbacks

FEAR STREET®
R·L·STINE

Final Grade

A Parachute Press Book

AN ARCHWAY PAPERBACK
Published by POCKET BOOKS
New York   London   Toronto   Sydney   Tokyo   Singapore

This book is a work of fiction. Names, characters, places and incidents are products of the author's imagination or are used fictitiously. Any resemblance to actual events or locales or persons, living or dead, is entirely coincidental.

AN ARCHWAY PAPERBACK *Original*

An Archway Paperback published by
POCKET BOOKS, a division of Simon & Schuster Inc.
1230 Avenue of the Americas, New York, NY 10020

Copyright © 1995 by Parachute Press, Inc.

ISBN: 0-671-86838-1

First Archway Paperback printing April 1995

10 9 8 7 6 5 4 3

FEAR STREET is a registered trademark of Parachute Press, Inc.

AN ARCHWAY PAPERBACK and colophon are registered trademarks of Simon & Schuster Inc.

Cover art by Bill Schmidt

Printed in the U.S.A.

IL 7 +

Final Grade

chapter

1

*L*ily Bancroft smoothed back her thick black hair and forced herself to take a deep breath. If you don't calm down, she told herself, you're not going to get anywhere.

She stared across the desk at her social science teacher. How can I convince him? she wondered. What can I say?

"Please, Mr. Reiner," she began in as polite a tone as she could manage. "Could you just listen to me for a few minutes?"

The handsome, young teacher took off his wire-rimmed glasses and raised his blue-gray eyes to her. The overhead fluorescent light flickered, casting an eerie greenish glow across his face.

"Okay, Lily," he said with a thin smile. "I'm listening."

Lily dropped her test booklet on his desk and pointed to the top of the page, where the teacher had scrawled a big red B.

"I—I don't understand my grade. I've gone over the entire test," she told Mr. Reiner. "The first ten multiple choice questions were all perfect."

"That's true," the teacher agreed quietly.

"On the next five questions," she went on, "the essay questions, I answered everything you asked for. There's not one place where you've marked a question wrong."

"Also true," Mr. Reiner said, his expression blank.

"I don't get it," Lily told him. "If nothing was wrong, why did you give me a B?"

"You're correct that there's nothing *wrong* with your essay questions," Mr. Reiner replied. "And they're good answers—B answers. But you didn't bother to go the extra step. You didn't write really *excellent* answers—the kind that deserve a top grade."

Lily frowned at him. Most of the other girls in the senior class at Shadyside High had a crush on the good-looking young teacher. But not Lily. She thought he was arrogant and conceited.

Not to mention difficult. Before taking Mr. Reiner's class, she had never had problems with a teacher.

Lily gritted her teeth in frustration. "In your other class, Alana Patterson wrote practically the same thing I did, and you gave her an A."

"But you, Lily, are enrolled in *honors* social science," he pointed out. "I told the entire class at the beginning of the year that this course would be more challenging than most. I have a different standard for honors students. I expect more, and I grade accordingly."

"But that's not fair!" she protested shrilly.

Mr. Reiner shrugged. "Hey, no one said life is fair."

"Mr. Reiner," she pleaded, "I've worked so hard in this course all year. You know I have. I was up practically all night studying for this test. And if . . . if the grade stays a B, there's no way I'm going to get an A in the course."

"Are you trying to make me feel sorry for you?" he asked. "Am I supposed to think that's the end of the world?"

Above their heads the light flickered and buzzed.

Mr. Reiner scowled. "That light's acting up again," he murmured. He stood up and circled the area underneath the fluorescent lamp, trying to get a better look.

Who cares about a stupid light fixture? Lily thought angrily. What's his problem? The most important thing here is my grade—and he's not even listening to me!

She had the sudden urge to grab the stapler on Mr. Reiner's desk and heave it at the fixture. *That* would get his attention!

"There must be something I can do," Lily continued, unable to keep her voice steady. "Some way I can get a better grade."

Mr. Reiner adjusted his glasses and fixed his icy gaze on her face. "The whole point of an honors course is in its title. It is an *honor*. You are expected to work harder. You are expected to do more work than the average student. I'm afraid your test"—he tapped his forefinger on the papers—"just doesn't do the job."

The fixture let out another buzzing sound. Mr. Reiner glanced overhead again. "I've been waiting for three days for the maintenance man," he complained. "If he doesn't come soon, I'm going to get a ladder and fix it myself."

"Please, Mr. Reiner," Lily begged again. "Can't you give me an A minus? That would raise my average enough to get an A in the course."

"I do not 'give' grades, Lily," he said coldly. "I only award them—if they are earned."

She stared angrily at him, swallowing the lump in her throat. What a jerk, she thought. How could he be so heartless? He's determined to make my life miserable.

"Is that your final answer?" she asked.

"Sounds like it to me," Mr. Reiner replied, smiling.

He was smiling! This whole thing was a big joke to him.

Lily closed her eyes and squeezed back the tears that threatened to fall.

I can't let him do this to me, she thought. I can't. I can't!

She plunged across the desk.

"Hey—what—?" the teacher cried out in surprise, raising his hands to shield himself.

"That was your last chance!" Lily shrieked. She shoved his arms away and wrapped her hands around his throat.

Yes! she thought. Yes!

Furiously she squeezed with all her strength. Tighter. Tighter . . .

The teacher clawed at her hands, trying to break free.

No use.

His eyes bulged. His distorted face darkened to purple. Hoarse choking sounds escaped his throat.

"You should have changed my grade!" Lily shouted.

She let go as Mr. Reiner gave one last gurgle and fell across the desk. Dead.

chapter

2

"**I**s there anything else?"

"What?"

"Lily, you're just standing there staring at me. Do you have anything else to ask me?"

Lily's eyes flickered open. Mr. Reiner sat gazing smugly at her from across the desk.

She shook her head to clear it as she took a few steps backward.

I can't believe I did that. I was so desperate to get him to change the grade, I actually pictured myself reaching across the desk and strangling him.

The teacher stared at her, waiting for a response. But Lily couldn't get out another word. She snatched up her test paper and ran from the classroom.

She had to get away, had to escape from Mr. Reiner's piercing eyes.

Did he have any clue about what she was really thinking?

As she raced into the crowded hallway, someone called out her name. "Lily! Hey—Lily!"

She whirled around. Her best friend, Julie Prince, hurried to catch up with her. A concerned expression filled her brown eyes. "You okay, Lily? You look terrible."

Lily shook her head. "I . . . I want to murder him, that's all."

"Don't say things like that!" Julie cried. Then she lowered her voice. "Murder who?"

Too late, Lily remembered that those words weren't just a casual remark to Julie. Four years ago Julie's older brother had been killed during a robbery at the grocery store where he worked.

Julie talked about her brother all the time. She couldn't shake the memory of his violent death.

"I'm sorry," Lily apologized, squeezing her friend's hand. "You know I didn't really mean that. I'm just so furious at Mr. Reiner."

Julie's expression softened. "What happened?"

"He gave me a B on the social science test. Can you believe it? There's not one thing marked wrong, but he gives it a B."

Julie shrugged. "It's only a test, Lil."

"Easy for you to say," Lily replied bitterly. "If I can't get him to raise the grade, I'll probably get a B for the term and have to kiss the college scholarship goodbye."

"Even without an A in social science you've got terrific grades," Julie reminded her. "You'll probably get offered lots of scholarships. Your mom and dad will still be proud of you."

Lily shook her head. "There's only one scholarship that really matters to me and my parents—the Shadyside Honors Scholarship. But it only goes to the valedictorian—the person who graduates with the best grades in the whole class."

"Well, it's not that late in the term," Julie encouraged her. "You can still make an A. Now come on, walk me to the library before it closes."

Lily followed her friend down the long, empty hall to the school library. They walked in silence, their shoes thudding on the hard floor. Lily couldn't stop thinking about Mr. Reiner and that frightening fantasy she had in his classroom.

Lily wanted to lighten up about her grades, but she couldn't help herself. Being valedictorian and getting the scholarship that came with it mattered a lot to her. It was the only way she'd be able to go to a really good college after graduation.

Both of Lily's older sisters, Becky and Melinda, had gone to Shadyside High—and both had graduated as valedictorian. Number one. Top of the class.

Lily wanted to be there too.

Talk about pressure! Lily's parents expected it of her—and she expected it of herself. This was the last semester of her senior year. And up till now she'd gotten A's in every course.

Why couldn't Mr. Reiner see that he was about to ruin her life? Why couldn't he wipe the smirk off his face and just change the stupid grade?

"I'll just be a sec," Julie said, interrupting Lily's thoughts as they reached the library. "I need to return these mysteries. They're overdue."

Lily smiled in spite of her foul mood. Julie had a huge stack of books tucked under her arm. Ever since her brother died, Julie devoured mysteries. While other kids hung out watching MTV, Julie went through mysteries as if they were bags of popcorn.

"I'll wait out here," Lily said. She stared glumly at her reflection in the display case outside the library door.

Usually she liked the way she looked, but not today. Her face appeared pale beneath the dark halo of her hair, and shadows circled her blue eyes.

Too much studying for social science, she thought bitterly. With nothing but a B to show for it.

Lily gasped as a hand clutched the back of her neck.

"Alex!" she shrieked.

Her boyfriend, Alex Crofts, grinned at her. "Gotcha!" He flicked a stray dark curl off his forehead and shrugged. "I couldn't resist, Lil. You were totally spaced out."

His grin faded as he noticed Lily's glum expression. "Hey—what's your problem? You mad at me or something?"

"No." Lily relaxed and forced a smile to her face. "It's Mr. Reiner. I can't get him to change that test grade I told you about."

"Bummer," Alex muttered.

"Yeah. Tell me about it," Lily replied. "I went in to talk to him. It—it was like he enjoyed giving me a bad grade. Like it gave him a thrill or something."

"Don't get crazy," Alex scolded. "Reiner's tough, but he's a good teacher."

Lily stared at Alex for a second. Was she the only one in the senior class who thought Mr. Reiner was a total creep?

"I can't explain it," she said finally. "I have this feeling about him—"

"I found some new mysteries," Julie called out, interrupting Lily. She appeared from the library, her arms full of books. Abruptly her happy expression dimmed. "Oh, hi, Alex."

Lily frowned. Last year Julie and Alex had gone out for several weeks. Both of them said it was no big deal, just a couple of dates. And six months ago, when Alex and Lily first started dating, Julie said she was happy for them.

So why is Julie acting so weird now? Lily wondered.

She hated feeling awkward around her best friend and her boyfriend.

"There you are!" Scott Morris's loud, cheerful voice filled the hallway. Scott was the editor of *The Forum,* the school literary magazine. "Hey—practically my whole staff. Why aren't you guys in the office? We have a deadline day after tomorrow."

"We were on our way," Alex spoke up.

"Hey, Scott," Julie chimed in. "I have this great idea for a book review. I read a really cool mystery last week."

"A mystery?" Scott said, pretending to be shocked. "Can't you read something normal for a change, Julie? Well, come on, we'll talk about it."

He turned the corner toward the magazine office, then glanced back, his green eyes meeting Lily's. "You coming too?"

"Uh, no." Lily hesitated, then glanced away. She liked Scott a lot, but sometimes he was so intense. It made her feel uncomfortable. "I have to work this afternoon."

"I thought you were off Wednesdays," Alex protested.

"I'm supposed to be. But Agnes is sick and I promised to fill in for her."

"What about that essay you were going to write for the next issue?" Scott asked.

"It's almost finished," Lily replied. "I promise I'll get it in on time. See you guys later."

She waved as her friends disappeared around the corner. With a sigh she headed in the opposite direction, to the front of the school.

The last thing Lily felt like doing today was working at her uncle's drugstore. But there was no way she could ever miss a day of work. She had been working at the drugstore for the past two years, ever since her mother's stroke.

With her mother ill and unable to work, it was up to

Lily to earn money for college. Even if she did get the Shadyside Honors Scholarship, she'd need money to cover expenses like books and clothes.

When Lily reached the street, the North Shadyside bus pulled out from the stop in front of the school. She began to run, but the bus rumbled away.

"Oh, wow!" she moaned. Couldn't anything go right today?

She stood for a moment, not sure whether to wait for the next bus or start walking the two miles to the store. Either way, she would be late.

"Lily!"

She turned back to the street and spotted Graham Prince sitting at the wheel of his father's sea-green Porsche.

"Hey—whussup?" He flashed her his best Graham Prince smile, all sparkling teeth and flashing blue eyes. "Want a ride?"

Lily usually avoided Graham. She'd known him since grade school, but they'd never gotten along. Graham was very cute and very smart—and he knew it. But he was Julie's cousin, so sometimes she had to put up with him.

Today she was almost glad to see him. She needed the ride. "Thanks," she said, opening the passenger door and sliding into the luxurious white leather bucket seat. "I do need a ride."

"Where to?" Graham asked.

"Bob's Drugstore. In the Old Village," she said.

"Your uncle's place, right?" Graham revved the engine, then pulled smoothly out into traffic. "Good old Uncle Bob. Everyone calls him Uncle Bob, right? I always thought Uncle was his first name."

"Ha ha," Lily replied flatly.

"So what's up? How's school? How's life?" Graham demanded.

"Fine," Lily said.

Her mind flashed back to the B she'd gotten on the social science exam. She wasn't about to tell Graham about that.

After all, Graham was her main competitor for valedictorian. In fact she'd been competing with him for best grades since sixth grade.

"Just *fine?*" Graham smirked. "Wow. You're real talkative today."

Lily tried to change the subject. "What about you?" she asked, gazing out at the passing front yards. "How are your classes?"

"I'm acing everything," he replied with a wave of his hand. "History, business math, biology—all A's. I guess we're still tied for first place."

"I guess so," Lily muttered. "Are you ready for the trivia contest?"

Next week at school was the first round of a statewide trivia contest. The winner would go on to compete against other students in the area, then maybe to compete at the state level.

The state finals winner would be awarded a five-hundred-dollar prize.

Lily hoped to win. The money would definitely help her college fund.

"I never lose a game of Trivial Pursuit," Graham

bragged. "Never. There's no way I can lose this contest."

She tuned out as he rambled on and on about what a trivia king he was.

A few minutes later Graham eased the car into a spot in front of the store. Lily sighed with relief. "Hey—thanks for the ride," she said, hopping out.

"Anytime," Graham replied. He honked the horn twice as he drove off.

What a mega-jerk, Lily thought. She couldn't stand the idea of Graham graduating number one in their class—or winning the contest. He was so confident. So smug.

Didn't he ever have problems like she did?

I can't let him be number one, Lily thought with new determination. I just can't.

"You're welcome," Lily said with a smile. The elderly woman customer thanked her and tottered out of the store.

Lily closed the register and settled back on her stool behind the counter, trying to focus in on her calculus homework. Usually math was her best subject, but the drugstore was so busy tonight she hadn't been able to concentrate on schoolwork.

She glanced at her watch. Ninety minutes till closing time. She couldn't wait. Uncle Bob was in the back, filling prescriptions. As soon as he finished, she could start getting ready to go home.

She turned another page in the textbook and started working on a new set of problems. When the bell over the door jangled, she pasted an automatic smile on her face and glanced up at the next customer.

A young man stood in the doorway, wearing a tattered denim jacket and a menacing expression.

"M-may I help you?" Lily asked.

"Yeah, you sure can," the young man replied, his eyes darting nervously from side to side.

He pulled out a small silvery pistol from his jacket pocket.

Lily gasped in fright. Her entire body froze.

He stepped forward quickly, up to the counter, and raised the pistol to Lily's face. "All the money. Give it to me. Hurry."

chapter

3

N*o!*

No! Lily thought. *This isn't happening.*
This isn't happening to me!

She glanced over her shoulder, toward the back of the store.

Where was Uncle Bob? Still in the back room?

What should I do? she wondered. Scream? Drop down below the counter? Give him the money?

"Hurry," the man urged, waving the shiny pistol. "Open the drawer."

Lily hit the Open button on the register. Her hands trembled as she began removing stacks of bills.

"Hey—!" the deep voice of her uncle boomed from the back of the store. "What's going on here?"

The robber spun around, pistol in hand. "Don't move!" he ordered Lily's uncle.

Obediently Uncle Bob stopped in the middle of the aisle. His face quickly drained of color as he realized what was going on.

"Now move slowly—over there!" The robber pointed with the gun to the counter where Lily was working. "That's it. Move slowly and nobody gets hurt."

His eyes locked on the robber, Uncle Bob approached the counter. Lily backed against the shelves to make room for him, her heart hammering in her chest.

The robber had a dark, wild look in his eyes. Fear. Mixed with hatred.

He's going to kill us both, she thought. Her mind flashed on Julie's brother. Julie's poor dead brother.

Yes. He's going to kill us. I can see it.

"Empty the cash drawer. Hurry." The pistol was trained on Uncle Bob's chest.

Lily moved back toward the cash register, but Uncle Bob stopped her. "I'll take care of it," he whispered.

With one hand he pressed the release on the cash drawer. With the other he quickly opened a small drawer below the register.

"Hurry!" the robber snarled. "I don't have all night!"

Lily stood trembling behind her uncle. She saw him slide his hand all the way into the drawer. And she saw him remove a small gray pistol.

"Hurry! Don't you know how to hurry?"

"Forget it!" Uncle Bob shouted angrily. He brought up the pistol and jammed the muzzle into the young man's chest. "Now put down that gun."

Lily held her breath.

No one moved.

The big clock ticked loudly behind her.

The robber backed away from Uncle Bob's gun. He kept his pistol raised. He let out an angry growl. "I'm going to kill you both," he said.

chapter
4

I don't want to die, Lily thought. *I don't want to die like Julie's brother.*

"Drop it," Uncle Bob insisted, holding the pistol firmly. "I know how to use this thing. Drop it!"

The young man hesitated. His eyes darted crazily back and forth.

Lily could see him thinking, frantically trying to decide what to do.

Please drop it! she urged silently.

Please listen to Uncle Bob. Please—drop the gun.

She let out a long *whoosh* of air as he slowly lowered his pistol.

Now she could see only fear in his eyes.

"Don't move!" Uncle Bob ordered him. "Lily, call the police."

Lily froze. Her entire body trembled.

"Lily—the police," Uncle Bob repeated quietly but firmly, his pistol trained on the young man. "Take a deep breath. Step over to the phone. Call them."

Before she could move, the robber turned and bolted for the door. "I'm outta here!" he shouted.

He reached the glass door as a tall boy with red hair started to enter.

He shoved the boy hard with his shoulder and dived out into the street.

"Rick! Watch out!" Uncle Bob cried.

The red-haired boy glanced from Lily's frightened face to the gun in Uncle Bob's hand. Without saying a word, he spun out the door and took off after the robber.

"Call the police, Lily!" her uncle shouted again. "Quick."

Lily followed his instructions and punched 911 into the phone. She reported the incident to an operator, who promised to send officers to the scene.

Her knees trembling, Lily turned to her uncle. "I can't believe it!" she cried. "He pointed the gun right in my face."

Uncle Bob tucked his gun back in the drawer and shut it. He turned to Lily and wrapped her in a long hug. Even with his arms around her, Lily couldn't stop trembling.

"Sorry this happened, honey," he said. "I'm so glad you're okay." He started toward the door. "Can you see Rick Campbell? He's my new delivery boy. Why did he run out? I hope he doesn't try to mess with that guy."

Lily stared at the glass storefront. "I don't see him." Then she dropped down on a stool to wait for the police. "I didn't know you had a gun in here," she said.

"I started keeping it about five years ago when crime went up in this part of town," Uncle Bob explained. "Luckily, this is the first time I've ever had to take it out of the drawer."

A moment later Rick burst back into the store, red-faced and breathing hard. "I lost him in the alley," he reported. "Are you two all right?"

"We're fine," Uncle Bob replied. "But you should be more careful, Rick. You shouldn't take off after armed robbers. You could get killed."

Rick shrugged. A macho shrug.

Uncle Bob turned back to Lily. "Are you feeling any better?"

"I'm still shaky," she answered honestly. "I can't stop seeing that shiny pistol. I can't stop thinking about . . . about Julie's brother."

The sound of a siren filled the air. Lily saw flashing red lights outside as a squad car pulled up to the curb.

Two dark-uniformed police officers hurried into the store. "I'm Officer Peyton," the taller one announced. "You reported a robbery?"

While Lily and her uncle told the officers what happened, Lily kept glancing at Rick. He leaned against the perfume counter, staring intently at them. He had longish red hair and piercing blue eyes. Lily met his gaze twice, then had to turn away.

Uncle Bob stopped her. "Please, Lily, go home. You know you don't have to stay."

"Thanks, but it's no big deal—really," Lily said with a smile.

He looks so familiar, she thought. *Have I ever met this guy before?*

"This is the third attempted robbery on the street this week," Officer Peyton said, scribbling notes. "It sounds like the same guy. You'd better be extra careful till we catch him."

The two police officers ambled out. Three customers entered. Lily made her way behind the counter to wait on them.

Uncle Bob went back to filling prescriptions. Lily tried to act as if nothing had happened, but she still felt shaky and frightened.

The customers filed out. Lily looked up to see Rick standing at the electronics counter, his gaze still fixed on her.

She smiled uneasily. "I've never been in a robbery before," she said. "It—it was really scary."

He nodded. "Wish I'd grabbed the guy. The police will never catch him."

"I'm just glad no one got hurt," Lily replied softly.

Rick shrugged. "It looked to me like your uncle had things under control."

"Uncle Bob was amazing," she agreed. "He really scared that guy. I hope he never comes back."

She shuddered, then reached for her calculus book, determined to force her mind onto something else, something normal.

A few minutes later Rick crossed over to the counter. "What's that—algebra or something?" He leaned against the register.

"Calculus." Lily drew back a little.

"You go to Shadyside High?" he asked.

Lily nodded, keeping her eyes down on the book.

"I've heard that's a pretty good school," Rick told her. "I didn't like my school much."

Lily glanced up and smiled politely. Then she gestured at her book. "I'd better get these problems done."

"You doing anything after work?" Rick asked. "Feel like getting something to eat or something?"

"No, thanks," Lily told him. "I have to get home."

"You have a boyfriend?" Rick persisted.

"Actually, yes—I do." She frowned impatiently. Can't this guy take a hint?

"Lucky guy," Rick murmured. He backed away from the counter. "Well, hey—so we'll be friends. Okay?"

Lily felt some of her anger melt away. Rick seemed a little dense when it came to taking hints, but he had a nice smile. "Sure. Friends," she agreed. "But if you're a real friend, you'll let me finish my homework."

"Okay, okay," Rick replied. He made his way over

to a display of painkillers and toyed with an aspirin bottle for a moment. Then he set it down. "So, uh, Lily?"

"What?" she said. This time she didn't bother to hide her exasperation.

"Do you *like* studying?"

"Well . . . yes, I do," Lily replied, surprised by the question. "At least sometimes."

"That's cool," Rick said. "I'm just not into studying. That was my problem at Mattewan."

"Is that where you graduated from—Mattewan?"

"No. Actually, I dropped out. I couldn't handle a lot of the classes, you know? Well, maybe you *don't* know what it's like to have problems with classes."

Lily studied Rick for a moment. "Sure, I have problems," she said. "Everyone does." She briefly told him what happened that afternoon with Mr. Reiner.

"Whoa," Rick said, shaking his head. "Sometimes those young teachers are the worst. They think it makes them cool to jerk you around."

"I guess," Lily agreed. "He just doesn't understand how important the grade is to me."

"Sounds like *he's* the one with the problem," Rick said. "In fact—" He broke off as Uncle Bob came out of the back room.

"Rick, I've got the deliveries ready," Lily's uncle said.

"Well, I've got to go," Rick said. "Sure you don't want to hang out later?"

Lily shook her head. "I really have a lot of work to do."

"How about a ride home?"

"No, thanks." She waved goodbye and returned to the calculus.

By the time Lily prepared to close up the store, Rick still hadn't returned. She felt relieved. He seemed like a nice guy, but he was sort of a pest. And she didn't have time to hang around the store talking. She needed every spare moment to get her homework done.

She said good night to her uncle and hurried to the bus stop on the corner. The days were getting warmer, but the night was cool. A quarter moon hung lazily over the swaying treetops.

The bus arrived about ten minutes later. Lily climbed on and settled into a seat in the back. She opened her calculus book again and leaned over it, studying the problems.

A few minutes later she sighed in frustration. The bus was bouncing all over the road. She'd have to finish at home—even if it meant staying up all night.

The bus driver braked at the corner of Old Mill Road and Fear Street. Lily gathered up her books and stepped out. The streetlight at the corner was out, and the shadows seemed even darker and more menacing than usual.

Why doesn't someone fix that light? she wondered. She started toward home, glancing uneasily around her. The picture of the man holding the gun at her flashed back into her mind. She shuddered.

What if he is out here? What if he is waiting for me?

Crazy thoughts.

Why would he follow her home?

The wind picked up, and she pulled her sweater tighter around her shoulders. Two streetlights on the next block were out too.

What's going on? she wondered. Why are so many lights out on Fear Street?

Between the wind and the broken lights, the shadows on every corner seemed to move with a life of their own. A tall, skinny cypress tree across the street twisted in front of Lily like a tall ghost.

Stop it, Lily, she scolded herself. You've had a frightening night. But stop trying to scare yourself even more!

Her house stood only two blocks away. The night seemed to grow even darker as she approached it. The wind made the trees billow and shake.

As she crossed to her side of the street, she heard a rustling sound. Something—or someone—was sneaking through the bushes.

The robber?

Is it him?

Did he really follow me home?

Panic choked her throat.

Lily whirled around.

No one there. No one.

It's just the wind, she told herself. Just the blowing leaves.

She began to jog, then quickened to a run.

Almost to the corner now. Just another half a block.

I can make it. I know I can.

She gasped as someone stepped out of the bushes to block her path.

I'm trapped, she saw.

He's got me.

chapter

5

Lily's frightened scream rose over the wind.

She froze, her heart pounding.

The tall figure stepped out of the darkness.

"Lily—it's me!"

Lily squinted at a familiar face. "Alex?"

"I didn't mean to scare you. Are you okay?"

"I think so," she said. She let out a long shuddering breath and moved into his arms.

"What's the matter with you?" he whispered, his lips brushing against her hair. "Didn't you recognize me?"

"I'm sorry," she said. "It—it's so dark. There was a robber. At the store. I—I was so scared."

Alex pulled back and studied her face. "Huh? What are you talking about?"

"At the store," Lily repeated breathlessly. "A guy came in with a gun." She hid her face against his chest. "It was so awful."

"Lily, are you all right? Was anyone hurt?"

Lily shook her head. "My uncle . . . my uncle came out of the back room just as I was about to hand over the money in the register. He grabbed the gun he keeps in the store, and the robber took off." She shivered again. "If he hadn't come out . . ."

"Shhh." Alex held her tightly as she burst into sobs. "It's all right, Lily. You're okay now."

She cried quietly for a few minutes, then took a deep breath to calm herself. As she gazed around, she realized they were standing in front of Alex's house, less than a block from her own.

"Have you been waiting for me?" she asked, surprised.

"Yeah, I was," he replied. "I tried to study, but I couldn't concentrate. I was worried about you. You seemed so upset about Mr. Reiner."

Lily sighed. "Oh, Alex, I'm all right." She was touched that Alex cared so much. "I'm okay," she repeated, smiling up at him. "Really."

"Sure?"

"Sure. Want to walk me home?"

"That was the plan," he said. He wrapped his hand around hers and walked close beside her. Lily felt warmer and more secure now. With Alex walking beside her, the wind seemed gentler, the darting shadows less menacing.

They stopped at Lily's front walk. "Thanks again," she said, looking up into his calm gray eyes.

"I'll walk you up to the door," Alex said. They climbed the porch steps together.

Lily started to open the door, but Alex took her hand and gently pulled her back. "Don't go in yet," he whispered. "Let's sit and talk for a while."

Lily glanced longingly at the wicker loveseat in front of the picture window. It would be so great to be with Alex, to hang out talking for a while. But . . .

"I'd like to," she said, shaking her head, "but I've got to get in and study."

Alex's face darkened. "You always have to study. Or else you're at work. I hardly ever get to see you, Lily."

"I know," she replied softly. "I'm sorry. But I have to finish my calc homework. And my essay for the magazine is due. And the Spanish review quiz is coming up. Plus I have to start cramming for the trivia contest. I'd really like to win the five-hundred-dollar prize."

"Okay, okay." He pulled his hand away abruptly. But when he spoke again, his voice was softer. "Really," he repeated. "It *is* okay. I know how important school stuff is to you. But I wish you weren't so busy all the time."

"I'll try to make more time, Alex," she said. "I promise." She lifted her face to his and felt his lips on hers. They kissed, then he hugged her tight, as if he didn't want to let go.

She hugged him back, then pulled away. Alex quickly turned and stepped off the porch, taking long strides.

I'm so lucky, she thought, watching him make his way toward his house. Alex is such a good guy.

Lily inserted her key in the lock and pushed in the door. "Hi, I'm home," she called. She dumped her backpack and books at the foot of the stairs, then hurried into the kitchen.

Her father sat at the table reading a newspaper. He raised his eyes to her anxiously as she entered the room. "Lily! I'm so glad to see you." He stood up to hug her.

With his thick salt-and-pepper hair, broad forehead, and sparkling blue eyes, she'd always thought her father was a handsome man. But after Lily's mother had the stroke, he seemed to age so quickly. His hair had grown mostly gray, and deep worry lines creased his forehead.

"Bob called to tell us about the robbery. Are you okay, honey?"

"I'm fine," Lily told him quickly. The last thing her father needed to hear—on top of all his other worries—was that someone pulled a gun on her. "It was scary—that's all."

"Bob said you handled yourself really well."

She shrugged. "He's the one who saved the day." She smiled brightly and changed the subject. "What's for dinner? I'm starved."

"Your mom's sleeping, but she made you a meat-loaf sandwich. It's in the fridge."

"Yum." Lily poured herself a glass of milk and located the sandwich on the top shelf of the refrigerator. Then she sat down next to her father.

"Have much homework tonight?" he asked.

"Tons," Lily replied with a sigh. "I'll be working late tonight."

"We're so proud of you, Lily." He beamed at her. "Your mom and I know you're going to be valedictorian—just like your sisters. And with your mom being sick and all, it really gives her something to look forward to."

Thanks, Dad, Lily thought dryly. *Thanks for putting the pressure on.*

What if I don't finish number one?

What will that do to Mom?

"How are your classes going?" Mr. Bancroft continued. "How's calculus?"

"Actually, it's my best class," Lily replied. "I've made A's on all the quizzes so far."

"Good for you!" said her father. "And how about your other classes?"

"Oh, mostly okay," Lily replied vaguely.

"Does that mean there are some that *aren't* okay?"

"Well, there was this one test in honors social science," Lily said. "I . . . um . . . I got a B on it."

For a moment her father didn't answer. She didn't need to turn around to imagine his look of concern.

"I'm sure you'll be able to bring the grade up," he said after a moment. "Not that I'm pushing. It's just that we're so proud of you and your sisters," he added.

"We don't want to see you do less than you're capable of."

No. Not that you're pushing, Lily thought with more than a little sarcasm. She set down her glass of milk and forced herself to smile. "Right, Dad. I guess I'd better hit the books then."

She tossed the rest of the sandwich in the trash, then scooped up her books and took them upstairs. If Dad only knew how close I am to blowing my chance to be valedictorian, she thought unhappily.

It made Lily fume at Mr. Reiner all over again. Why couldn't he change her grade? Why?

Lily switched on her study lamp and settled herself at her desk. She finished her calculus problems quickly. Next came her Spanish homework.

She stifled a yawn as she began revising the essay for the literary magazine. It was a piece about the history of Shadyside High School.

She glanced at her watch. Almost midnight. If she weren't so tired, she thought, she would really enjoy working on this essay.

She had nearly finished writing when the phone rang. She jumped. Who could be calling this late?

She grabbed the receiver before the second ring, hoping the sound hadn't awakened her parents. "Hello?"

"Lily," whispered a muffled, breathy voice. "Lily."

"Yes? Who is it?"

No reply. Only slow, raspy breathing.

"Hello?" Lily repeated, trying to keep the panic out of her voice. "Who is it?"

"It's me," said a male voice.

"Who? *Who?*"

"Someone who knows you, Lily. Someone who knows everything about you. Someone who watches you all the time."

Thinking hard, her mouth suddenly very dry, she shifted her hand on the receiver.

"Who *is* this?" she demanded hoarsely. "Who?"

She heard a click on the other end.

Then silence.

chapter

6

As the morning bus pulled away from the Fear Street stop, Lily held in a yawn.

"Yo—Sleepyhead!" Alex exclaimed. "Time to wake up."

"Sorry," she replied, unable to keep the yawn in. "I was up really late, and then I couldn't get to sleep."

"Why not?"

She hesitated. For some reason she didn't want to tell Alex about the strange phone call. She felt a little foolish. She didn't want to admit she'd spent the whole night tossing and turning, wondering who made the stupid prank call.

"I couldn't get Mr. Reiner off my mind," she said finally. It wasn't the whole truth, but at least it wasn't

35

a lie. "I have to find a way to get him to change my grade."

"Forget about it, Lily," Alex said. "Everyone knows Mr. Reiner never changes grades."

"I think he will this time," Lily told him. "I had a great idea when I woke up this morning. I told you he said that he expects extra from the honors students. Remember?"

"Yeah, so?"

"Well, that's the answer. I'll offer to do some extra credit work to make up my grade on the test."

"Hey, Lil. It just *might* work," Alex agreed. "But don't count on it. Reiner's pretty strict about stuff like that."

"I have it all worked out," Lily told him. "I'll write an extra paper, or do an oral report, something that will show him I don't mind working harder. Then he'll feel comfortable about raising my grade to an A."

"Well, good luck," Alex replied. He gave her a solemn handshake.

She laughed.

Alex is so great, she thought. He can always make me laugh. Even when I'm as stressed out as I am now.

"I can't let my parents down," she told him. Her father's proud face flashed in her mind. "You know they're counting on me to be valedictorian. If Reiner won't change my grade, I—I'm doomed."

They climbed off the bus in front of the school. Alex waved goodbye, then jogged over to join a group of his friends near the basketball courts.

Lily hurried toward the front steps, eager to find

Mr. Reiner before homeroom. *I've been thinking about what you said, Mr. Reiner,* she rehearsed. *And I agree that I haven't been doing honors work. That's why I want to do some extra assignments, to take that extra step.*

She stopped at her locker to drop off the books for her afternoon classes. Two freshman girls stood at the corner of the hall, whispering to each other. Their lowered voices reminded Lily again of the strange phone call.

Who called her in the middle of the night? Was someone really watching her?

Stop thinking about it, Lily scolded herself. The call was a stupid prank. Some loser from school with nothing better to do.

She slammed her locker shut, then took a deep breath and headed down the hall to Mr. Reiner's room.

The door was shut, but she knew he would be there. He was known for getting to class early and staying later than most of the other teachers.

"Hi, Lily!"

Lily turned to see Lisa Blume, the editor of the school paper. "Lily—what's up?"

"Nothing much." Lily shrugged. She tried not to sound too friendly. Lisa always wanted to talk about the kids they knew. Who was going out with whom. Who was fighting and breaking up.

The last thing Lily felt like doing right now was gossiping. All she could think about was getting her talk with Mr. Reiner accomplished.

"How come you're here so early?" Lisa asked.

"I need to see Mr. Reiner about something," Lily replied.

Lisa nodded knowingly. "I heard about your problem with him. He wouldn't change your grade, right?"

Lily groaned to herself. If Lisa knew about her troubles with Reiner, the rest of the school did too.

"Does this mean Graham will make valedictorian?" Lisa asked. "I mean, you need an A in Reiner's class—right?"

"I'll get my A one way or another," Lily snapped.

Immediately she wished she could take back her sharp reply. But it was too late.

Now Lisa will tell everyone that I acted like a desperate nut over my final grade, Lily thought unhappily.

Lisa gave Lily a thumbs-up and backed off down the hall. "Well, good luck," she called.

Sighing, Lily turned back to Mr. Reiner's room and knocked on the door. Without waiting for an answer, she turned the knob and pushed the door open.

The first thing she saw was a ladder, positioned under the broken light fixture. Lily raised her eyes and saw that the long fluorescent bulb had been removed.

Had Mr. Reiner decided to change the bulb himself?

He probably went to the custodian's supply closet to get a new bulb, she thought. I'll wait right here until he comes back.

She set down her backpack on a nearby desk and walked over to the ladder behind Mr. Reiner's desk.

She let out a horrified gasp when she saw the bright red blood dripping off Mr. Reiner's desk. She followed the blood with her eyes. And found a body.

"Mr. Reiner?" she managed to choke out.

The handsome young teacher lay sprawled on his back near the desk. Blood soaked his hair. His mouth hung open. His eyes stared blankly up at Lily.

"No!" Lily cried. "No! Please—no!"

She lowered her eyes. She had stepped into a puddle of blood. The blood ran over the sides of her white sneakers.

Not my imagination this time, she realized, pressing her hands to the sides of her face.

Not my imagination.

This time he is really, truly dead.

chapter

7

*T*he day after Mr. Reiner's funeral, Lily went straight to her seat in his classroom without looking around.

She still hadn't recovered from the funeral. All through the service hardly anyone spoke a word to her. Whenever Lily raised her eyes, she saw people staring at her with accusing eyes—as if *she* had something to do with Mr. Reiner's accident.

Even Alex acted a little distant.

You're being totally paranoid, Lily, she scolded herself. *No one blames you for what happened. Everyone knows it was an accident. They just don't know what to say to you.*

But why did she feel so guilty?

True, she never liked Mr. Reiner. And true, she would have done almost anything to raise her grade.

But she never wanted anything bad to happen to him.

The memory of what she'd said to Julie that afternoon haunted Lily. *"I want to murder him."* That's what she had told Julie.

And Lisa Blume must have told everyone in school about how angry and stressed out Lily sounded the morning of the teacher's death.

Do they really think I pushed him off the ladder or something? Lily wondered.

My friends can't *really* think that about me—can they?

Mr. Reiner's classroom was silent, eerily silent. A few students whispered. No one spoke aloud.

Lily fished in her backpack for her notebook, keeping her eyes down. Mrs. Burris, the substitute, stood in front of the class.

Lily tried to push the terrible thoughts out of her head. She listened closely to everything the new teacher said as she outlined the course for the rest of the semester.

But sitting in this classroom only reminded Lily of finding Mr. Reiner's body. Of seeing his sprawled corpse, his pale face, his open mouth, his blank, lifeless eyes.

"We will have two more exams, and a term paper." Mrs. Burris's words cut into Lily's thoughts. She leaned forward to pay attention.

Two more tests and a paper? she thought.

With that much work, plus homework assignments, Lily would definitely have a chance to improve her final grade in social science.

A second chance!

Yes! she thought, feeling a little cheered for the first time in days.

Yes! Maybe I can beat out Graham for valedictorian, after all!

"Love-forty!" Scott called from across the net. "Come on, you wimps!"

Lily shut her eyes for a moment and concentrated as hard as she could. She tossed the ball into the air, swung her tennis racket back—and smacked the ball into the net.

"Oh, wow!" she cried. She took a deep breath and prepared to serve again. This one also fell short.

"Double fault!" Scott cried gleefully. "Game and set!"

Lily couldn't help laughing. "I'm sorry," she told Alex. "I don't know how I did that!"

"I can't believe you blew that point!" Alex said.

"Hey, it's okay," Lily said, giving him a playful shove. "We'll get them next time."

"We'd better," Alex muttered. It was her first free Sunday morning in a month. Lily had really been looking forward to playing doubles with Julie, Scott, and Alex.

She toweled off her forehead, then moved to the

shade on the sidelines. Julie was pouring cups of pink lemonade from a thermos.

"Sorry, guys," she said. "I just can't seem to get my serve going today."

"I can't believe it," Scott said. "Usually you've got a great serve. What happened?"

Lily shrugged. "Beats me. Guess I'm losing it."

Scott shook his head. "Weird," he said. "You're so competitive in school. But out here it's like you don't care if you win or lose."

"I guess I *don't* really care," Lily told him. "I guess for me tennis is just having fun."

"Well, me too," Julie chimed in. "But for me part of the fun is winning."

"Yeah. Right," Alex said, pouring himself a second cup of lemonade. "Winning isn't everything . . . but if you don't at least *try* to win, I mean, what's the point?"

"Okay, okay!" Lily laughed. "I guess I'll work on my killer instinct next set."

The instant she said it, she regretted it—especially when she saw Julie exchange glances with Scott.

Luckily, Alex quickly broke the tension. "Come on," he said, slamming down his cup of lemonade. "Let's go get them."

Lily and Alex won the next two games, then narrowly lost the last three.

"It's such a nice day. Anyone want to go biking?" Scott asked as he packed the thermos onto his bike rack.

"I can't," Julie said. "My family's going to my grandmother's for the afternoon."

"I can't, either," Lily told them. "I have to study."

"Oh, come on," Alex protested. "It's still early. You've got all day."

"Not really," Lily replied. "It's getting too close to the end of the term. I just can't take the time."

Alex scowled, then shrugged. "Whatever," he said. "I just wish you'd learn to take it easy once in a while."

"That's what I've been doing all morning," Lily replied. She waved to the others, then started to walk home.

When she reached the corner of Old Mill Road, she heard a honk. A car revved its engine, then stopped beside her.

"Hey, want a ride?"

She turned to see Graham Prince in his Porsche. "No, thanks," she called. "I'm almost home."

"Come on. Climb in," he coaxed her. "It's too hot to walk all that way."

"All that way? It's only two blocks!" She started to walk away, but Graham beckoned her over to the car.

Reluctantly she approached the gleaming Porsche.

"Hey, Lily." A teasing grin spread over his face. "You must be feeling pretty good now, right?"

"Excuse me? What do you mean?" she demanded.

"Well, now that Mr. Reiner is taking a dirt nap, maybe you'll get an A in social science." Graham let out a high-pitched laugh.

"I can't believe you said that!" Lily cried angrily.

44

"Hey, whoa," Graham said, cutting off his laugh. "Take it easy, Lily. It was just a joke. That's all." He pushed his glasses up on his nose.

"Not funny! How could you joke about a thing like that?" Lily demanded.

"Everyone knows how upset you were about that B you got on your test," Graham replied. "Lisa Blume told me you were ready to spit when you went in to see Reiner—right before you . . . right before you . . . found him."

"Leave me alone, Graham!" Lily shouted. "I don't like what you're thinking. I wouldn't kill someone to get an A!"

"Okay, okay."

"I mean it!" she cried. "Mr. Reiner had an accident. A horrible accident! If you think—"

"I said I didn't mean it!" Graham cried, raising both hands, as if in surrender. "You'd better lighten up, Lily."

"Leave me alone," she muttered.

"Hey—no problem," he replied coolly. He shifted the Porsche and roared off down the street.

Lily stood for a moment, watching him go. Her knees trembled. How could Graham say those things to her? What kind of monster did he think she was?

Did everyone in school think she had murdered Mr. Reiner?

That night, when Lily turned off her study lamp, the clock read a few minutes before midnight. She knew she should spend some more time getting ready for the trivia contest, but she was too sleepy.

I'll work harder tomorrow, she promised herself.

She changed into her pajamas and slipped into bed. As she closed her eyes, eager to get some sleep, the phone rang.

Startled, she grabbed for the receiver. "Hello?"

"Lily?"

Now she was wide awake. That voice again. The creepy whisper.

"Who is this?" she demanded.

"I know all about you, Lily," the voice whispered. "And I know that you got what you wanted. Didn't you?"

Lily didn't answer for a moment. She concentrated on identifying the voice. So familiar. So familiar . . .

"I know who you are!" she blurted out. "Why are you calling me? Tell me! Why are you doing this to me? Why, Graham? Why?"

Click.

chapter

8

"Hey, Lily!" Scott waved as Lily burst into *The Forum* magazine office. "Right on time."

"I rushed over after class," Lily said breathlessly. "I can't stay long. You said this meeting was important."

"It's our last chance to go over the final material for the magazine," he agreed, nodding. "Where's everyone else?"

"I saw Julie by the library," Lily replied. "She said she'll be here in a few minutes."

"This essay you wrote is excellent," Scott said, tapping his finger on the top page of Lily's essay for *The Forum*. "You really dug up great stuff about the early days around here."

"Thanks, Scott," Lily replied, feeling herself blush. Sometimes she found it hard to take a compliment.

She'd enjoyed writing the essay, even though it had taken time away from studying for the trivia contest and her regular homework.

"We go to press tonight," Scott told her. "Do you want to come down to the plant and watch it roll off the press?"

Luckily for *The Forum* staff, Graham's father owned a printing plant. He let the students print the literary magazine there one evening a month for practically nothing. Usually a few staff members went along to watch.

"Sure. I've never been to the printing plant," Lily said.

"Then you ought to go," Scott urged. "It's really interesting. The paper comes on huge rolls that feed between these cylinders. The cylinders print both the front and back of each sheet. When the printing is finished, the whole thing is cut into sheets and bound. All on one enormous press."

"Sounds cool," Lily observed. "I guess I can stop by for a few minutes before I start my homework. Is nine o'clock too late? That's when I get off work."

"Yeah. Come at nine," Scott replied. "That's when we usually get the thing rolling.

He sighed. "First, we have to choose the cover photo." He picked up a manila envelope and slid out a sheet of contact prints. "Take a look at these and tell me what you think."

Lily leaned over the table to see the photos. All the prints were shots of the school, taken at night with the moon gleaming off the roof.

"I think I like this one best." Scott pointed to one of the prints in a corner of the sheet. "What do you think?"

"That one's good," Lily agreed, leaning in closer so she could see better. "But I think my favorite is this one here, where you can actually see the moon." She lifted the contact sheet for a clearer view.

"Hmm," Scott said, examining it. He guided Lily's hand to bring the print closer to his eyes. "I see what you mean. You have a good eye, Lily."

Hearing a sound, Lily raised her eyes to the door. Alex stood there, an angry, intense expression clouding his face.

"Alex!" She automatically moved away from Scott. "Come look at these photos."

"No, thanks," Alex replied sharply. "You guys seem to be doing fine without me."

"We're picking the cover photo for the next issue," Scott explained. "Want to take a look?"

"Not really." Alex scowled. "I'm sure you'll go along with whatever Lily wants."

Oh, wow! Lily thought, staring hard at Alex. Is Alex actually jealous of Scott?

"They're here if you change your mind," Scott said, tossing the manila envelope on the table. He didn't seem to notice Alex's anger.

"I'm going to go take some copy into Mr. Henderson," Scott announced. He picked up a stack of papers and carried them to the magazine adviser's office next door.

"Alex, what's your problem?" Lily demanded as soon as they were alone.

"Huh? Excuse me?" Alex replied sullenly.

"You're acting like you're jealous of Scott!" she said. "I can't believe it."

"Well, why shouldn't I?" Alex shot back. "I know he's got the hots for you!"

"Don't be a jerk!" Lily snapped.

"Oh, Lily! You have such a good eye, Lily!" Alex exclaimed, mocking Scott.

"Alex, cut it out. I'm not interested in Scott. We're just friends, and you know it." She jumped up and threw her arms around his shoulders. "Come on, Alex. Shape up," she teased. She planted a kiss on his cheek.

Alex gave her a reluctant smile. "So which one of the photos do you like?"

The magazine staff meeting didn't end until six-thirty. Lily barely had time to catch the bus and get to her uncle's drugstore on time.

When she arrived, she found the store jammed with customers. Uncle Bob told her that it had been an unusually busy afternoon, and he'd probably need to spend most of the evening filling prescriptions.

Lily took her spot behind the counter. Since the robbery, she'd been nervous about being up front alone. But tonight was so busy, she didn't have much time to think about her fear.

Rick showed up at the drugstore at eight o'clock.

Things had quieted down, and Lily started doing some homework in between customers.

"Hey, Lily." Rick swaggered over to the counter. "How's it going?"

"I'm fine, Rick," she said, trying not to sound impatient.

"What's up with you?" He leaned his elbows on the counter, trying to see the book open on her lap.

"I'm studying," she told him. "And I still have quite a bit of work to do, so if you don't mind . . ."

"What are you studying?" Rick persisted.

"This happens to be Spanish," she said. "Now, please, Rick—if you'll just let me—"

"Is that the course you got the bad grade in?" Rick demanded. "The B?"

"That was a different course," Lily said. "Now, Rick, I really—"

"You know, I read about that teacher in the paper," Rick went on. "That Mr. Meiner . . ."

"Reiner," said Lily.

"Right. Reiner. The guy you were complaining about. He wouldn't give you a break, right?"

When Lily didn't answer, Rick dropped his voice to a whisper. "So what did you do, Lily? Give the guy a little push? You know. For extra credit?"

"That's disgusting!" Lily cried, straightening up. The Spanish book slipped off her lap onto the floor, and she bent down to retrieve it.

"Hey, whoa. Take it easy," Rick said. "I'm just kidding around. Just goofing on you a little. I didn't mean—"

"Look, Rick, I'm busy," Lily said sharply.

"When aren't you busy?" Rick continued to lean on the counter, gazing into her eyes. He reached over to touch Lily's hair. "Why don't you forget all this schoolwork and go out with me tonight? We can go wherever you want."

"I already told you I have a boyfriend," Lily said, pushing his hand away. "And I don't have time to go out anyway." She opened the book on her lap and stared down at it, deliberately ignoring Rick.

He grabbed her hand.

"Hey—you stuck up or something?" he rasped. "I only want to get to know you better."

"Leave me alone!" she cried angrily. She hopped off the stool and tried to pull away from him.

Rick moved away from the counter, raising both hands in surrender. "Hey, whoa. Don't get all sweaty. I didn't mean anything." He took another step back.

"Just back off," Lily snapped.

"Don't worry," Rick said. "Hey, sorry. Guess I came on a little strong. Don't say anything to your uncle, okay? I need this job."

Lily opened her mouth to reply—when the door to the back room opened and Uncle Bob stepped out. "Is everything all right?" he asked. "Who's shouting out here?"

Rick stared intently at Lily, his eyes pleading.

"It's all right, Uncle Bob," she said after a moment. "Rick and I were just kidding around."

* * *

At nine o'clock Lily left work and hurried to the printing plant to meet her friends. The scene with Rick still troubled her mind.

There's something kind of creepy about Rick, she decided. Last night she had been certain that Graham had made the prank phone calls. Now she wasn't sure.

Had it been Rick?

The printing plant was located in the middle of Shadyside's industrial section. It was housed in a large factory building on a block with several other businesses. All of them were dark and closed for the night, except for the printing plant.

A single streetlight cast a harsh yellow glow between the black shadows. Somewhere Lily could hear the wind scuffing trash along the abandoned street.

She crossed the street to the printing plant. Its large front door stood open a crack, and a faint light shone from somewhere in back.

Lily pushed the door all the way open. The smell of printer's ink filled the dark, deserted lobby. She heard low sounds from the back of the building and followed them through a short hall into a large room.

Under the bright lights Lily saw the enormous web printing press. The press stood nearly a block long, with a huge roll of paper on one end.

She squinted into the brightness, searching for her friends.

"Hey—where is everybody?" she wondered out loud.

She heard a rumbling sound.

The rumbling became a roar.

A rock slide? An avalanche?

Lily froze as a voice behind her called out a warning. "Lily—watch out!"

She spun around in time to see the tower of huge paper rolls tumbling toward her. In time to realize that she was about to be crushed to death beneath them.

chapter

9

With a thunderous roar the enormous rolls of paper crashed onto the floor.

Lily uttered a shriek.

Tried to dive out of the way.

A shock of pain roared through her body as one of the heavy rolls clipped her leg.

Sent her sprawling to the floor.

"Noooooo!" A horrified howl escaped her throat. Ignoring the pain, she crawled frantically over the concrete floor.

With a desperate lunge she flung herself behind a steel pillar. Turned. And watched the heavy rolls bounce and tumble past.

"Are you all right, miss?" A bearded, middle-aged

man rushed to her side. "They didn't hit you, did they?"

Lily tested her leg. Sore but not broken. "I—I'm okay," she replied shakily. Her heart was pounding so hard she could scarcely breathe. She inhaled deeply to steady herself, then let the man help her to her feet. "What happened?"

The man scratched his thinning hair. "Those rolls shouldn't have been stacked like that. I don't get it."

"Lily, are you okay?"

"What happened?"

"Were you hit?"

Scott, Alex, and Julie surrounded her with concerned questions.

"I'm all right," she told them, staring to feel a little calmer. "Really I am."

"Are you sure you weren't hurt?" Lily recognized another voice. She turned to see Graham approach. A thin smile crossed his face.

Was he actually glad she'd almost been crushed?

No. She shook her head to chase away the thought. Of course not. Why am I thinking such things?

"I'm fine. Really," she assured them all. She pushed her black hair back off her perspiring forehead.

"This is Mr. Jacobson, my father's night foreman," Graham told her, pointing toward the bearded man. "He's been helping us get set up for tonight's printing."

"Except now we'll have to put it off while I get this mess cleaned up," the foreman groaned, shaking his head.

"That's all right," Scott told him. "How soon can we come back?"

"We'll be ready for you again tomorrow," Mr. Jacobson said. "But let me caution you kids. A printing plant isn't some kind of amusement park. As you just saw, it can be a very, very dangerous place."

"Right, Mr. Jacobson," Scott agreed. "Thanks a lot. We'll see you tomorrow."

"I don't believe that happened!" Julie exclaimed once they reached the front of the building. "You could have been killed, Lily."

"I'm fine," Lily reassured her. "Only I'm disappointed we didn't get to see the magazine get printed."

"Actually, I'm not sure we could have printed tonight, even without the accident," Alex told Lily. "We were having trouble with the big press. Mr. Jacobson said he'd get it working, but it kept sticking."

"He didn't know what he was doing," Graham said, joining the others on the front walk. "Sometimes it takes a while to get going."

Lily flashed him an annoyed glance. Why was Graham always so sure of himself?

"Come on, guys," Scott said. "Let's go to Pete's Pizza. I'm starving."

Lily hesitated, thinking about her homework. Then she thought, *Hey, I was nearly killed tonight.* "Good idea. Let's get some pizza!" she exclaimed.

* * *

By the time she reached home, it was almost eleven. Lily was too tired even to look at a book.

The trivia contest was scheduled for tomorrow. Lily knew she should go over her notes again. But she couldn't bear the thought of reading a single word.

She stretched out on her bed. What a day, she thought, sighing. Her leg throbbed now. She was sure she'd have a bruise by tomorrow. At least nothing else can happen tonight, she thought as she dozed off.

The phone rang.

"Oh, no," she murmured. "What now?" Her heart pounding, she picked up the receiver. "Hello?"

It was the whispery voice. "Lily? Is that you?"

"Who are you? What do you want?" she demanded angrily.

"I want what you want," the hushed voice told her. "And I'm going to help you, if you'll let me. Please, Lily, please let me help."

Lily slammed down the phone and yanked the cord out of the jack. There. Now he couldn't call again. She wasn't going to let this jerk—whoever he was—upset her one more time.

But long after she'd disconnected the phone, the chilling voice lingered in her ears.

Who is it? she wondered. Who?

When Lily entered the auditorium for the contest the next afternoon, she felt confident and calm.

"Good luck," Alex whispered, giving her a quick kiss on the cheek.

"Thanks." Lily climbed onto the stage and took her seat with the half-dozen other finalists.

As Lily had expected, the first part of the contest was easy. But an hour later only three contestants remained—Lily, Graham, and Susie Dawson, a transfer student.

The moderator was Mr. Spencer, an assistant principal. "What was the name of the first mayor of Shadyside?" he asked Susie to begin the next round of questions, which focused on local history.

Susie sat, thinking for several seconds. Finally she shrugged. "I don't know," she replied with a sigh.

"I'm sorry," Mr. Spencer said. Shaking her head, Susie stepped down from the stage and took a seat in the audience.

Mr. Spencer turned to Graham. "Do you know the name of Shadyside's first mayor?"

"Robert Briggs," he answered quickly.

"That's right!" Mr. Spencer said. "Congratulations, Graham. Congratulations to both of you. Let's move on to the next round."

Lily forced herself to concentrate. Why did Graham always have to be in the finals of every contest she was in? Couldn't he mess up just once?

She gazed out into the audience again. Most of her friends were still there, including the entire staff of *The Forum*.

Her eyes stopped on Alex, and he flashed her a wink. Sitting next to him was Julie, and next to her, Scott. From the looks on their faces she could tell that they were all rooting for her. It felt great to have so much support—especially since she'd felt so uncertain about her friends after Mr. Reiner's death.

Mr. Spencer paused to discuss a question with another teacher. Graham turned to Lily. "This is fun, don't you think?" he whispered. "It's better than sitting in class."

"Yeah. It's kind of fun," Lily replied. What else could she say?

Mr. Spencer cleared his throat, getting back to business. "Lily," he said. "The early settlers built two bridges over the Conononka River that are still standing. What are they?"

"The River Road Bridge," Lily said, naming the first one that popped into her head. "And the . . . the . . ."

She had to stop for a moment. It would be so much easier to think if Graham weren't sitting so close. She felt a moment of panic as the name slipped out of her mind. "I know it, I definitely know it," she said. "I just can't . . ."

"Take your time," Mr. Spencer said soothingly.

"Yeah, take your time, Lily," Graham whispered sarcastically. "We've got all day."

Lily felt so angry, she felt like pushing Graham off the stage. But the flash of anger also cleared her head. "The Mill Bridge!" she declared.

"Right!" Mr. Spencer turned back to Graham. "Now, for your next question . . ."

Lily tuned out and tried to calm herself. If you want

to win this contest, you've got to forget about Graham, she told herself.

Both of Lily's sisters had won the school trivia contest when they were seniors. Becky had even made it to the state finals. Lily knew she could do the same—if she put her mind to it.

"That's right!" Mr. Spencer was congratulating Graham for another correct answer. "The two of you are doing very well. Let me just get the next round of questions." He began fishing around in a manila envelope.

"By the way, Lily," Graham whispered. "I checked my midterm grade average at the office this morning. Guess how I did?"

"Shh!" Lily said, trying to ignore him. Couldn't Mr. Spencer see what Graham was doing? Couldn't he see that Graham was trying to blow her concentration?

But the moderator was busy searching through his envelope for the next set of questions.

"Am I a genius or what?" Graham whispered. "I have straight A's so far. That's A's, not A minuses or B pluses."

"Way to go, Graham!" Lily replied sarcastically. She felt her throat tighten with anxiety.

Straight A's meant that Graham was ahead of her for the term. Even if she could raise her grade in social science, she might not get more than an A minus at this point.

"What about you?" Graham persisted. "Any minuses or pluses in there?"

"Are you keeping a scorecard?" Lily snapped.

"Only making conversation," Graham replied, grinning his toothy grin.

Again Lily felt anger welling up in her. It was only a game to Graham, she realized. He didn't need the money. He just wanted to be valedictorian to beat her. She wouldn't even mind losing to him so much if she thought it meant anything to him.

She took a deep breath and waited for her next question. "What was the major occupation of the original founders of Shadyside?"

The original founders? Lily started to answer "Farmers." But it seemed so obvious. Maybe it was a trick question. Why would they have such an easy question in the final round?

Beside her, Graham fidgeted in his chair.

Maybe the question referred to the first people who moved into Shadyside *after* it had become a town— not the first settlers, Lily thought.

"Railroad men," she answered finally.

"I'm sorry." Mr. Spencer shook his head. "That's incorrect. If Graham can answer the question correctly, he will be the winner and will represent Shadyside in the state contest."

Lily's stomach clenched. I blew it! she thought miserably.

"That one's easy," Graham gloated. "They were farmers."

"You're right!" Mr. Spencer cried. "Congratulations, Graham, you are our Shadyside High trivia champion."

Graham beamed proudly. The audience applauded. He gave them a wave. Then he turned to Lily, his smile still stuck in place. "Hey, better luck next time."

"Congratulations," Lily muttered. She couldn't bear to see his smug grin. She jumped up, turned quickly, and bolted down the steps and out of the auditorium.

She could hear Alex and Julie calling her name. But she didn't want to see them. She wanted to be alone.

"Better luck next time." How could Graham be such a creep?

I'll walk home, she decided. It will give me time to cool down.

As she headed away from school, the final question from the trivia contest repeated in her brain. How could she have been so stupid? The answer—farmers —was totally obvious.

With a sigh Lily made her way into an alley behind a row of houses. The alley was a shortcut that led past a wide, empty lot.

Lily was halfway past the empty lot when she became aware of footsteps behind her. She turned around—and saw Rick running toward her.

"Lily! Hey—wait up!" he called out breathlessly.

She leaned against the chain-link fence beside the alley and waited for him. "Rick, have you been following me?" she demanded.

"No. No way," he replied, breathing hard. "I always take this shortcut when I'm in this neighborhood. I was on my way to a delivery and I recognized you."

She started walking again. He followed.

"I don't see any packages," she said suspiciously.

"I made my last delivery," he replied. "You don't mind if I walk with you—do you?"

She hesitated, still feeling uncertain about him. "Okay," she agreed. "But I don't have a lot of time. I have to get home."

Rick grinned. "Oh. That's a real change," he said sarcastically. "Usually you've got *plenty* of free time for me."

She forced a laugh. Maybe Rick isn't so bad, she thought.

As they walked along, he talked about working at the drugstore. "I like working for your uncle. I don't make a lot of money, but your uncle Bob treats me real well." He glanced sideways. "You're quiet today. So how's school?"

What did Rick care? Lily thought. He doesn't even go to school. "Why do you want to know?" she demanded.

"I don't know," Rick said with a shrug. "I thought maybe I could help you somehow."

At those words Lily froze. That was what the telephone caller whispered.

She wheeled to face Rick. "Have you been calling me late at night?"

He didn't hesitate. "Yes," he replied.

chapter

10

"*I*t *was* you! I knew it!" Lily screamed. "You've been calling, then hanging up?"

"Yes," Rick confessed. "I always hang up before you answer. I just don't have the nerve to talk to you, I guess."

"Don't lie to me, Rick!"

"I'm not lying," he replied sharply. "I called you twice. Both times I let the phone ring two or three times and then hung up. I swear."

She stood, staring at him. "I don't believe you," she said coldly. "From now on just leave me alone, okay?"

With those words Lily took off toward Division Street. She didn't stop running until she was sure she had left Rick far behind.

* * *

As she studied that night, Lily kept waiting for the phone to ring. But she received no whispered call.

By the time she climbed into bed, she felt more certain than ever that the caller had been Rick. I'm glad I confronted him, she thought. Now he'll leave me alone.

When Lily arrived at school the next day, she found a small group of students gathered around the big bulletin board by the school office.

Lily pushed her way to the front. The midterm grade rankings had been posted. As Graham predicted, he was head of the class—and Lily was number two.

"Oh, wow!" she moaned to herself. She kept reading the rankings, as if staring at the list would change the numbers.

Mrs. Burris had finally given her an A minus. But it wasn't enough to keep Graham from edging a tiny percentage point ahead of her.

It's not fair! she told herself as she hurried to her first class. Every term she took harder classes than Graham. But that didn't matter when it came to the rankings.

For the rest of the day Lily tried to put the class ranking out of her mind. But by the after-school magazine meeting, it was still all she could think about.

As soon as Lily walked into the meeting, Alex handed her some pages. Lily had almost forgotten that

Scott planned to try again tonight to print the magazine at the press. All the staff members were supposed to go over the copy for last-minute changes.

"I think I found a mistake in your essay, Lily," Alex pointed out. "There seems to be a line missing in the second paragraph. What do you think?"

She quickly scanned the page. Nothing appeared to be wrong. "It looks fine," she snapped.

Alex drew back as if he'd been bitten. "I'm only trying to help. What's up with you?"

"Sorry, Alex," Lily said. She suddenly felt like crying. She struggled to hold back the tears. "I didn't mean to be a jerk. It's just the class rankings."

She turned away. She didn't want anyone to see the tears that brimmed in her eyes. "How am I going to tell my parents that Graham is valedictorian? They'll be so disappointed in me."

Scott walked over to the editing table. "There's still plenty of time till the end of the semester, Lily," he said softly. "Something could change, you know."

Lily shook her head grimly. "It's a done deal. Graham's going to be our valedictorian—unless he suddenly flunks out or falls off a cliff or something."

"Being second isn't exactly terrible," Julie chimed in. "Your friends won't care. I don't think your parents will be as upset as you think. I really don't."

"You don't understand, Julie!" Lily cried shrilly. "No one understands!" She rushed out the door and down the hall to the girls' bathroom.

How will I ever break the news to my parents? she

wondered, leaning over a sink and staring at herself in the mirror.

How will I ever tell them?

That night very few customers came into the drugstore. Uncle Bob let Lily leave early.

As Lily packed up her books, she decided to head to the printing plant to watch the magazine get printed. After her outburst at the meeting, she felt embarrassed to see her friends. But at least she could apologize to everyone.

From the outside the plant appeared totally dark. A hand-lettered sign posted on the front door said, "Be back at 9:30, M. Jacobson."

Lily glanced at her watch. It was twenty till nine. Guess I'm too early, she thought.

She turned the doorknob and the door sprang open.

That's weird, she thought. Why would Mr. Jacobson leave the front door unlocked?

She let herself in and switched on a small lamp by a table in the reception area. Maybe she could sit here and get some homework done, she decided.

As she dropped her backpack on the table, a steady hum droned through the building. Lily gazed around. It must be the press, she decided. Maybe they started printing the magazine after all.

In the back of the building she saw a faint glow of light.

"Mr. Jacobson?" she called.

No answer.

She made her way to the huge room that housed the

big printing press. As she walked, the hum grew louder. She heard a rumbling, clattering sound.

To Lily's surprise, the press *was* running.

The big wheel of paper unrolled rapidly, feeding paper through the rollers. The huge press rumbled and clacked. A defeaning sound.

Holding her ears, Lily stepped closer, hoping to get a look at the pages of the magazine rolling off the big machine.

But as she leaned forward, something hot and wet splattered her face.

"Hey—!" She wiped her cheek with her finger.

And studied her hand, puzzled.

Red smears.

Red ink? Why were they printing the magazine in red ink?

Lily rubbed another smear off her cheek.

And studied it again.

No, she realized. Not red ink.

Blood.

chapter

11

"N₀₀₀₀!"

Lily uttered a terrified moan as more of the hot red liquid sprayed over her face, dripped down the front of her T-shirt.

Where was it coming from? Where?

From the rolling press?

With mounting horror Lily wiped the blood from her face. Stepped closer to the printing press.

Whoa.

The press wasn't running as she had thought. The big paper wheel was jammed.

Jammed by . . . jammed by . . .

"NOOOOOO!" Lily's hoarse scream echoed through the vast plant.

The paper wheel was jammed by a head and shoulders.

Graham's head. Graham's shoulders.

"Graham—!" she choked out. "Are you alive? Are you still alive?"

She moved behind the press. She tugged at his waist. She pulled frantically.

"Are you alive? Graham? Are you?"

She tugged and tugged at his limp, blood-soaked body.

One hard tug—and the huge paper wheel moved.

It spun slowly. Slowly.

And the body came free.

Lily heard the crunch of bones beneath the moving wheel.

And saw a river of bright blood pour down the side of the press, puddling loudly on the concrete floor, on the cuffs of her jeans, on her shoes.

With a terrible thud Graham's crushed, broken body rolled onto the floor. His lifeless, blood-soaked face stared up at the ceiling.

I . . . can't . . . breathe . . . Lily realized.

I'm . . . choking . . . choking . . . can't breathe . . .

Her legs gave way, and she crumpled to the floor.

Lily opened her eyes. Alex stared down at the mangled body next to her. He was shaking her shoulders.

Then he too began to scream.

Scott and Julie were right behind Alex. Lily heard their cries of horror and shock.

Lily pulled herself up to a sitting position. I fainted, she realized. How long was I lying here?

Scott ran to call the police. Julie knelt by the press, sobbing at her cousin's side.

"How could it happen?" Alex murmured. "How? How could Graham get caught in the press?"

He stared down at Lily. "And how did you get all that blood on you?"

Lily stared up at him, struggling to find words.

What is going on? she asked herself. First Mr. Reiner and now Graham. Why were all these people around her suddenly dying?

Why?

"Aren't you going to eat?" Lily's mother asked the next morning at breakfast.

Lily shook her head. She was still in shock. Graham's lifeless face, the gruesome sight of his crushed body, had haunted her all night.

"Just a few bites," Mrs. Bancroft urged. "After what you've been through, it's important for you to eat, honey. Keep up your strength."

Lily dipped her spoon into the bowl of granola crunch and forced herself to swallow a few bites. Then she heard Alex's car out in the driveway.

"See you later, Mom," she said. She stood up and placed the still-full bowl in the sink. "I've got to go."

Before her mother could protest, Lily kissed her quickly on the cheek and grabbed her backpack.

"Good morning," Alex said as Lily climbed into the

front seat. He leaned over and gave her a hug. "How are you feeling?"

"I'm not sure," Lily replied grimly. "How about you?"

Alex's face was unusually pale, and he had dark circles under his eyes, as if he hadn't slept much, either.

"I've been better," he muttered.

On the drive to school Lily closed her eyes and tried to relax. But all she could think of was what had happened last night and the questions nagging at her brain.

How did Graham get trapped in the printing press?

Was it an accident? The police seemed to think so.

Or was someone responsible for Graham's death?

Lily's throat tightened as she thought back to yesterday, to reading the class rankings.

She had been so angry. So upset. She had wanted to kill Graham.

This is all my fault, she thought. If I hadn't wished for Graham to die . . .

A sob escaped her throat and Alex glanced sideways. He squeezed her hand.

"It's because of me," she told him. "I was so worried about a stupid grade. And now Graham is dead."

"Lily." Alex shook his head. "Don't be ridiculous. You can't blame yourself for what happened. The police say Graham probably got too close to the machine. Even if you didn't like him very much . . ." Alex's voice trailed off.

Lily stared through her tears at Alex. She knew he was trying to reassure her. But she saw a flicker of doubt cross his eyes.

A loud honk startled Lily. Alex cursed as a carload of kids swerved in front of them, cutting them off.

"Hey—what's their problem? Jerks!" Alex shouted.

Lily recognized them. Seniors. Friends of Graham's.

One of them pointed at Lily and Alex. The others turned around to stare at Alex's car through their back window.

Lily ducked her head. Graham's friends probably think it's my fault, she thought, suddenly feeling cold all over.

They probably think I killed Graham so I could be valedictorian. That's what everyone will think when they find out I was the one who found Graham.

Just as I found Mr. Reiner . . .

For the rest of the ride, she stayed huddled in the passenger seat without saying another word. In front of the building she quickly kissed Alex goodbye, then hurried to homeroom.

On her way Lily passed the school office, and her eye fell on the class rankings. The thought flitted through her mind: *I'm number one. I'll be valedictorian.*

Once this fact would have made her jump for joy. Now she felt only emptiness and a dull fear.

The sky was slate gray. Drizzle slicked the concrete as Lily climbed the steps of the redbrick church where

Graham's funeral was being held. A cold wind whipped open her dark linen jacket. She gathered it tightly around her, then hurried into the church.

The suffocating, sweet fragrance of flowers filled the room where Lily waited in line to sign the guest book. Julie's mother and some of Graham's other relatives stood in an alcove, their eyes red from crying.

The pews were nearly filled by the time Lily got into the chapel. She took a seat on the aisle next to an overweight woman she didn't know. She recognized several solemn-faced classmates in the pews, some of them already sobbing into handkerchiefs.

At the front of the room sat a long, white coffin, piled with yellow and white flowers. Lily gazed at it till it dissolved in a blur of tears. Graham's death still felt unreal—more like a dream than the terrible truth.

The organ began to play a sad, slow march. Then the minister stood up. After a short prayer he began to speak about life in the midst of death and the tragedy of a young life cut off in its prime.

Then the mourners were invited to file past the closed coffin at the front of the room. Row by row, they stood, then began a slow march up the center aisle to the coffin, and then back to their seats.

When it came time for Lily's aisle, she forced herself to her feet. Her knees shook so hard she wasn't sure she could even stand. But she followed the overweight woman and the other people in the aisle up toward the front, where the casket stood.

As Lily neared the casket, her knees trembled harder.

I'm sorry, Graham, she thought. *So sorry. It's true I didn't like you. But I never, never, never wanted anything like this to happen.*

The overweight woman stood in front of the casket. She bowed her head and murmured a few words, then walked on.

Now came Lily's turn.

As she approached the casket, she heard a sharp, creaking noise.

Slowly the lid of the casket began to open.

"No!" she gasped, moving back a step.

The lid swung wider, wider, until she could see inside.

On a white satin cushion lay the pale, still form that had once been Graham. The corpse was dressed in a formal black suit.

Graham's face had been heavily made up. The cheeks were bright pink. But the rest of the skin was tinged with an inhuman green. One eye had sunk deep into its socket.

Slowly, slowly, as Lily stared in shock, Graham's corpse pulled itself up.

With a hideous groan the corpse pointed a long, bony finger at Lily.

The dry, purple lips opened slowly, popping stitches that had held the mouth closed.

The yellowing eyeball rolled, deep in its socket.

"It's her!" the corpse rasped. "She's the one!"

chapter

12

*L*ily couldn't move. Couldn't scream.

The corpse's purple lips closed silently. But Graham continued to point an accusing finger at Lily.

As she gaped in horror, the face began to change. Graham's features appeared to melt away, to fade. The entire body faded into the shiny white cushion inside the coffin.

Lily buried her face in her hands. When she raised her eyes, the coffin lay closed.

She blinked. Once. Twice.

She realized the coffin had been closed the entire time. She had imagined the whole frightening scene.

Feeling numb, she moved on, back to her seat. She scarcely heard the rest of the service.

Why do I feel so guilty about Graham? she asked

77

herself over and over. It's true that I wanted to be number one in the class, but I never wanted anything bad to happen to him.

Or did I?

After the service and the burial, everyone was invited to Julie's house for coffee and cake. Lily dreaded having to face Graham's relatives and friends. But she knew she had to go. Julie was her best friend. Lily had to be there—for Julie's sake.

Lily sighed. Only a few years ago Julie's brother was murdered. Now poor Julie had lost a cousin, too.

When Lily arrived, Julie stood with her parents and Graham's parents at the front door, greeting the mourners. Both Julie and Graham's mother dabbed at their eyes with handkerchiefs.

Lily hugged the parents and told them how sorry she was. Then she approached her friend. "I'm sorry, Julie," she murmured.

Julie gave a quick, tearful smile, then turned away quickly to talk with someone else.

Lily jerked back as if she'd been slapped. Why was Julie acting so cold? Did she blame Lily too?

Lily walked over to the table where drinks were being served. She wished she could run home and escape these strangers as well as her own overwhelming guilt.

"Hi, Lily." Scott stepped in front of her.

"Oh, hi, Scott," Lily said, happy to see a friendly face.

"I think Julie's really upset," he said gently.

Lily stared at him for a second. Had he seen the cold greeting she had received from Julie?

As Lily stood talking with Scott, she saw Graham's mother and another woman move over to the refreshment table. "He was such a handsome boy," Lily heard the other woman say. "You and Robert must have been so proud of Graham."

Mrs. Prince nodded. "We were very lucky. Graham was a wonderful son. And he was feeling so excited about everything too—finishing high school, being valedictorian . . ." Her voice choked, and she struggled to compose herself. "I . . . I can't believe he's gone."

The other woman gathered Mrs. Prince in a hug. Lily watched as she softly whispered something in Mrs. Prince's ear.

Then Graham's mother's eyes flicked over to where Lily stood with Scott. Her eyes bored into Lily's, and Lily jerked back involuntarily, sloshing some of her ginger ale onto Scott's shirt.

"Oh! Sorry!" Lily cried.

But Scott paid no attention to the wet spot spreading on his white shirt. "What's wrong, Lily?" he asked gently. "Are you okay?"

She shook her head, not trusting herself to speak. Then she backed away, grabbed her jacket from the hall closet, and ran out of the house.

It was still raining, but Lily scarcely noticed. She splashed blindly through the puddles on the sidewalk until she reached the familiar steps in front of her house. She yanked open the door and raced up to her room.

Lily flung herself onto her bed and cried hard for a long time.

"Please let this be a dream," she murmured over and over. "This can't be happening to me."

Finally Lily had exhausted all of her tears. She sat up and reached for the black handbag her mother had lent her for the funeral. She opened it, searching for a tissue to wipe her wet eyes.

Inside the small bag Lily felt something hard and sharp. That's weird, she thought. She didn't remember putting anything like that in the bag.

She shook out the contents of the purse, then stared in shock at the object lying on her bed.

There on her white bedspread sat a pair of dark, horn-rimmed glasses.

Graham's glasses.

The glasses he wore the last time she saw him alive.

chapter

13

With a hoarse cry, Lily tossed the glasses against the wall.

How had they gotten into her purse? Who had put them there? Why?

Lily's whole body trembled.

Someone has played a very cruel joke, she told herself.

Bang!

She jumped before she realized it was the front door slamming shut. Were her parents home? No. Her father wasn't due back from work for hours. Her mother had a doctor's appointment this afternoon.

Did I lock the front door? Lily wondered. She'd rushed upstairs after the funeral in such a crazed state, she wasn't sure about anything she'd done.

She listened hard.

Footsteps.

The heavy thud of someone climbing the stairs, one by one.

"Who is it?" she called weakly.

She sat up alertly on the corner of her bed. "Who's there?" she repeated.

No answer.

And then a familiar figure filled the doorway.

"Scott!" she cried, relief flooding over her. "You scared me to death! Why didn't you knock?"

"I did knock," he said. "But no one came to the door. The door was half open, so I let myself in." He narrowed his eyes, studying her face. "You okay, Lil? You left Julie's house so quickly."

"I'm doing a little better," Lily replied. She stood up. "Hey, it was really nice of you to come check on me."

"I was worried," Scott told her.

Alex is right about Scott, Lily found herself thinking. *Scott would definitely like to be more than friends.*

Lily realized she was glad. Right now she needed people to care about her and not be suspicious of her.

"I—I just couldn't take it. At Julie's house, I mean," Lily stammered.

Scott crossed the room. He bent over and picked up something from the floor against the wall. Then he turned back to Lily, a puzzled expression on his face.

"Graham's glasses," he said, staring hard at Lily.

"I don't know how—" Lily started.

"Don't worry, Lily," he interrupted her. "It will be our secret."

"You don't understand, Scott," Lily protested. "I don't know where they came from. I found them in my purse, but I didn't put them there. You've got to believe me!"

"Calm down, Lily." Scott was still staring hard at her, tapping the glasses against his palm.

"You have to believe me, Scott!" she insisted. "I didn't put them there!"

"I know," Scott said softly.

He took a few steps toward her, his eyes locked on hers. "I know you didn't put the glasses there," Scott whispered. *"I did."*

chapter

14

"*H*uh? You *what?*" Lily cried, stunned. "You put the glasses there? What are you talking about, Scott?"

Scott finally lowered his eyes. He took another step toward her. "I meant exactly what I said," he said softly. "I put the glasses in your bag, Lily. I did it at Julie's house. I wanted you to find them."

Lily dropped back onto the bed, her head spinning in confusion. What was he talking about? Why on earth would he do that?

"But where did you get them?" she demanded. "Why did you want me to find them?"

"So you'd know what I did," Scott answered. "So you'd know everything I did for you."

A chill went through Lily. "Did what?" she asked, her voice shaking. "Did *what* for me?"

Scott frowned. He shook his head unhappily. "I thought you knew," he said, slapping the glasses harder against his open palm. "I did exactly what you wanted. I killed Graham for you."

"Oh nooooo," Lily moaned.

"Oh, *yes!*" Scott declared. "I killed him. It was easy, really. I got the idea after Mr. Reiner's accident. It's so simple, isn't it, to make a death look like an accident?"

"Scott, you don't know what you're saying," Lily protested in a trembling voice.

"Oh, yes, I do." Scott beamed proudly. "After Mr. Reiner died, I started thinking. I knew you had a much better chance of making valedictorian."

He began to pace back and forth in front of the bed, twisting the glasses in his hand. "Except for Graham. He was such a jerk, always competing with you. So that night I told him to meet me at the printing plant at nine. I knew the foreman always took his dinner break then."

"And then—?" Lily asked.

"When Graham got there, I told him I was having trouble with the press. I said I thought it was jammed. He leaned over to take a look, and I shoved him into it."

"No—please!" Lily shrieked.

"Accidents happen all the time, Lily. Remember yours—when the paper rolls tumbled down and almost killed you? Now why wouldn't everyone believe Graham had one too? But he wasn't so lucky, huh?"

"Stop!" Lily yelled. She didn't want to hear another word. She pressed her hands over her ears to block out the sound of his voice.

"Listen to me!" Scott cried. He grabbed her wrists and pulled her hands away from her head. "Don't tune me out! You wanted Graham out of the way more than anyone! Admit it!"

When she didn't answer, he added softly, "I did it for you, Lily."

Tears streamed down Lily's face as she stared at him with revulsion. Scott had killed Graham. And he'd done it for her.

"I wasn't sure how to tell you," Scott said, still holding on to her wrists. "That's when I got the idea of putting the glasses in your bag. I knew how grateful you'd be when you realized what I had done for you."

"Grateful?" Lily repeated numbly.

"Yes," Scott replied excitedly. "After all, no one else would do so much for you. No one else cares for you as much as I do."

Lily shuddered. "How could you think I wanted you to kill Graham? How could you think that?"

"It was obvious," he replied. "Everyone knew Graham was your main rival. Besides, I could tell what you really wanted when we talked on the phone."

"What do you mean?" Lily said. "We've never talked on the phone."

"All those times I called you late at night."

Lily gasped. *"You* were the one? It was you who made those awful phone calls?"

"I like hearing your voice," Scott confessed, blushing. "I knew you'd be up late, studying. You always work so hard. Even though you didn't say so, I could tell that you were miserable. And it was all because of Graham."

"But that has nothing to do with you," Lily snapped. "That was between Graham and me."

"Haven't you been listening to anything I said?" Scott cried. "I did it for you. Because I want you to be happy. Because I care about you so much, Lily." He was breathing hard now, his face bright red, his eyes wild and excited.

"I—I love you," he blurted out.

Lily felt sick inside. Scott loved her? That's why he killed Graham?

"I've always loved you," Scott continued heatedly. "Since grade school, you've been the only one I've cared for."

"Grade school?" Lily echoed. "How come you never asked me out?"

"I never could get up the nerve," Scott admitted. "You always had a boyfriend. I've been so jealous of Alex these past few months. But all that's over now."

He's crazy, Lily realized, watching Scott talk. *He's totally messed up.*

I have to get help, she told herself. I have to find a way to distract him while I call the police.

"I'm sorry, Scott. I never knew you felt that way about me," she said carefully, thinking hard.

"All these years, I've just been waiting for the right moment to tell you," Scott said. "And now I'm so happy. Because now we can be together."

Lily fought off a wave of nausea. "Well, I'm glad you told me all these things." She stood up shakily.

"Where are you going?" Scott demanded, his voice suddenly suspicious.

"I'm—I'm—I'm just going downstairs for a moment," she said. "I'm thirsty. Do you want a soda?"

"I'll come with you," he replied. "Now that you know the truth, I don't want us to be apart again, even for a moment."

Lily forced herself to smile as she led the way into the kitchen. She'd have to think of another way to get away from him.

She reached into the refrigerator and pulled out two Cokes. "Here," she said, thrusting them at him. "Why don't you open these, and I'll get glasses from the dining room."

Without waiting for him to answer, she slipped into the dining room and headed straight for the phone in the family room. Her hand shook as she punched in the first two numbers of 911.

She was about to punch the last 1 when Scott's hand clamped down on her wrist again. "What are you doing, Lily?" he demanded. His eyes flashed with anger.

"I'm just . . . just making a call," she said.

"You were calling the police, weren't you?"

"No, I—"

"Don't lie to me, Lily!" he snapped. "Remember I

know you better than anyone. I can tell when you're lying. You don't believe in our love, do you?"

"I—I—"

He pulled her away from the phone and twisted her head around so she was facing him. "I know this is all very new to you. You don't understand yet, but you will."

Then he leaned in closer, pinching her face between his fingers. "Don't even think about it, Lily!" he warned. "Don't even think of turning me in. Remember—I've already killed once!"

chapter
15

*L*ily's mouth dropped open. She realized her entire body was trembling with fear.

I'll never get away from him, she thought.

He led her by the hand back into the kitchen, then handed her one of the sodas.

"Relax, Lily," he told her. "Have some soda and calm down. Everything has changed now, do you understand?"

Lily nodded. Everything *had* changed. Her life would never be the same.

"Now I've explained to you why I killed Graham," Scott continued casually. "I did it for you. I did it because you wanted me to—even if you won't admit it."

"I *didn't* want you to!" Lily insisted shrilly.

"Oh, I know better, Lily," Scott replied, smiling. "I know everything about you. I know everything you're thinking. You're still thinking about calling the police, aren't you?"

Lily didn't answer. She stared at Scott, at his wild eyes, his excited expression.

"You are," he said. "I know you are. But you can forget it. You can forget turning me in. Because if you do—your life will be ruined."

"What do you mean?" she choked out.

"Think about it," he replied flatly. He took a long drink of cola. "If you say *anything* to *anyone,* I'll tell them that it was all your idea. I'll tell them that you and I planned it together."

"You wouldn't do that!" Lily cried.

"I'd have to," Scott told her. "And everyone would believe me. After all, you have a motive. With Graham dead, you're the class valedictorian. Besides, a lot of people already think you killed Mr. Reiner."

"Scott, you can't be serious!" Lily gasped. "No one really believes I'd kill a teacher and Graham just to be class valedictorian."

Scott shrugged. "You were the one to find both bodies. Now, isn't that a bit of a coincidence?" He paused, obviously enjoying the effect his words had on her. "And I also can tell how I found Graham's glasses in your bedroom."

"No!" Lily shrieked. "I'll hide them. I'll destroy them. I'll—"

"Forget it," he snarled. "I have them now, and I'm going to keep them as insurance. But I won't need insurance, will I? You'll never tell anyone, will you, Lily?"

Lily shuddered. How would her parents react if Scott carried out his threat? If he told police that Lily was a murderer?

Her father would be heartbroken. And her mother's recovery from the stroke had been slow enough. News like this would devastate her, maybe even kill her.

But you're innocent! a voice inside Lily cried. *Don't let him do this to you!*

Then another more insistent voice argued: Being innocent doesn't matter, Lily. People will believe Scott. People will *want* to believe that you killed Mr. Reiner and Graham.

"I need to think about this," she murmured, feeling dazed, confused.

"That's fine," Scott said. "I understand you're a little upset now. But, Lily, remember. I did it for you. I did it so we could be together." He reached out and gently stroked her arm.

Lily jerked back.

His touch made her feel sick.

"I need time, Scott," she told him. "Please go now. I want to be alone."

"All right," Scott said calmly. "I'll go—for now. But don't forget, Lily. You owe me. You owe me everything."

Scott made his way out the front door. Lily didn't turn around.

What am I going to do? What am I going to do?

She sat in the kitchen, staring at the clock over the stove, watching the second hand roll silently, smoothly around.

What am I going to do? What am I going to do?

The question repeated endlessly in her mind.

The second hand continued to circle. An hour went by. Two.

She still didn't have an answer.

"Who can tell me the name of the president of Peru?"

Mrs. Burris stood at the front of the class, her eyes scanning the rows of students. "No one?" Her eyes came to rest on Lily. "Lily, what about you?"

"I . . . uh . . . I don't know," she stammered.

A frown crossed Mrs. Burris's face. "Lily? Really?" she said. "Didn't you read the assignment?"

"Yes, I did," Lily replied. "But I don't remember."

Mrs. Burris went on to another question, and Lily stared down at her desk. She had read the assignment, late last night after work.

But schoolwork suddenly seemed so unimportant and trivial. Her mind was on other things. Like Graham's murder. And Scott's terrible confession.

On the way to her next class, she passed Scott in the hall. He gazed at her intently. Then he flashed her a smile.

As if the two of them shared a wonderful secret.

Leave me alone! Lily thought miserably.

Just leave me alone!

But she knew that Scott would never do that. Never.

Unless . . .

Unless . . .

Unless she could figure out a way to make him.

chapter

16

Scott was already waiting in the magazine office when Lily arrived for the after-school meeting. She was the first to show up. Carefully she avoided his eyes and sat by the window, as far from him as possible.

"Why don't you sit closer, Lily?" he said. "I can hardly hear you way over there."

"I need some air," she said. She stood and pulled open the window. Before Scott could say anything else, Alex came in, followed by Julie.

"Hi, guys," Alex said. "I hope this meeting isn't going to last long. I've got a million things to do after school."

"Me too," Julie said. Lily glanced over at her friend.

It was the first time she'd bumped into Julie since Graham's funeral. For a second their eyes met, then Julie turned away.

"I wanted to talk about planning our next issue," Scott said. "It will be the last one of the school year. I thought we should make it a tribute to Graham."

"Great idea!" Julie's face lit up and she clapped her hands together.

"I think so too," Alex agreed. "Maybe we could even have a poem about him in it."

"Lily?" Scott turned his eyes to her. "What do you think? Do you like the idea of dedicating the issue to Graham?"

Lily narrowed her eyes. He's so sick, so cold, she thought bitterly. How does he have the nerve to make a suggestion like that?

Scott murdered Graham. He murdered him. Now he wants to dedicate the magazine to him.

"Sure," she muttered.

"Well, the main thing is we all agree," Scott said cheerfully, acting as if Lily had been as enthusiastic as everyone else. "I'd like everyone to write something about Graham. I'll write the lead article myself."

Disgust swept over Lily. Now Scott wanted to write a tribute to Graham?

He's actually enjoying this, she realized.

Scott went on to discuss some other business about the magazine, but Lily tuned out.

"All right," Scott said after a few minutes. "That's about it. Lily, can you stay for a few minutes? I have some things to discuss with you."

"Sorry," she said. "I promised my uncle I'd come in to work a little early."

Scott scowled angrily. But there wasn't anything he could say in front of the others.

"Come on, Lily," Julie spoke up suddenly. "I'll give you a ride to work. I've got some things I want to talk over with you anyway."

"Sure. Thanks, Julie," Lily replied, surprised by her friend's offer. She grabbed her books and followed Julie out to the parking lot.

"It's so sweet of Scott to have a tribute to Graham," Julie said to Lily as she started up the car. "I can't wait to tell my aunt about it."

"Yes, it is nice," Lily commented flatly.

Julie glanced at Lily, then concentrated on maneuvering the car out of the student parking lot, onto Park Drive. "Anyway, the main reason I wanted to talk to you is that I owe you an apology."

"Apology? For what?" Lily asked.

"I know I haven't been a very good friend lately," Julie replied. "It's just . . . you're always so busy, and when you are free, you hang out with Alex all the time." Julie shrugged. "It sounds stupid, but I guess I've been jealous."

Lily swallowed hard. So this is what's been bothering Julie? I had it all wrong.

Lily had been convinced that Julie somehow blamed her for Graham's death.

"You don't have to apologize," Lily told Julie. "I know I'm never around. It's hard for me to do anything after school with my job and everything else

I'm trying to do." She shook her head. "Actually, I think Alex is pretty fed up with me too."

Julie hesitated. "That's not the only thing on my mind."

Lily turned in the passenger seat, studying Julie's face.

"Ever since . . . ever since the night we found Graham," Julie continued, "I haven't been able to sleep or eat. I keep thinking about what happened." Her chin quivered. She kept her eyes straight ahead on the road.

"Me too," Lily replied.

Julie took a deep breath. "I think I've figured out what really happened to Graham. I—I think he was murdered."

"Huh?" Lily gasped.

"I know what the police and coroner believe," Julie said. "That Graham's death was an accident. But I don't buy that. Graham's father owned the printing plant. Graham had been around the printing press his whole life. There's no way he could have an accident like that."

"Anyone can have an accident," Lily said carefully.

"Not Graham," Julie insisted heatedly. "You know what he was like. He was so smart, so clever. He always knew what he was doing."

"I think you've been reading too many of those murder mysteries," Lily murmured dryly.

"I can't believe you're saying that!" Julie exclaimed. "I thought you of all people would understand why I feel this way. Or do you think—" She stopped. "Oh,

Lily, you don't think I suspect that *you* had anything to do with it, do you?"

Lily felt her face turn red. "Of course not. Why would I think that?"

Julie started to say something, then stopped. She eased the car to a stop at a traffic light. "Because . . . you know, because of what everyone's saying. How weird it is that you found both Reiner and Graham. But I don't believe any of those crazy rumors," Julie added quickly.

Lily shrugged. "I know what people are saying about me. And I'm trying my best to ignore it." She sighed. "So, who do you think murdered your cousin?"

"I don't know for sure," Julie said. "But I have some ideas."

Lily held her breath as Julie continued. "I couldn't do anything about my brother's murder. But this time it'll be different. I'm going to find out who murdered my cousin—if it's the last thing I do."

As she got ready for bed that night, Lily thought again about what Julie had told her.

If Julie was truly planning to investigate Graham's death, what would happen? What if she figured out it was Scott?

Lily didn't even want to think about what Scott might do or say if Julie accused him.

The phone rang, startling her from her troubling thoughts.

"Hello?" she said warily.

"Lily, it's me."

"Hi, Scott."

"You don't sound very happy to hear from me."

"What do you want?"

"Now, is that any way to talk to the person who cares about you so much?" he asked. "I thought you understood, Lily. I thought you understood that we're meant to be together—forever."

"I do," Lily replied, struggling to sound sincere.

She'd decided that the only way to deal with Scott was to pretend to go along with him—at least until she could figure out a solution to this mess. "But I don't think we should talk a lot or be seen together," she continued. "People might get suspicious. After all, it hasn't been that long since Graham's body—"

"That sounds like a pretty lame excuse," Scott interrupted. "You're trying to get rid of me, huh?"

"I'm only being careful," Lily whispered into the phone, glancing toward her bedroom door. "Besides, what about Alex? I can't just stop seeing him."

"Why not?" Scott demanded.

"Because—because we've been going together for six months," Lily stammered. "He knows me really well, Scott. If I suddenly start acting different, he'll know something is wrong. He'll suspect something's up."

"He doesn't know you as well as I do," Scott insisted. "Break up with him now, Lily. I want you to be with me."

"Soon," Lily said carefully. "But not yet."

"I've been very patient," Scott said. "But I don't want to wait much longer."

"We have to be careful," Lily told him again. "Some people are already suspicious."

"Like who?"

"Like Julie," Lily replied without thinking. "She thinks that Graham was murdered."

"Does she?" he replied casually. "Let her think it. There's nothing she can do."

"Don't be too sure," Lily said. "She's smart. And she says she's going to find out who did it."

"Really?" Scott paused. When he spoke again, his voice sounded menacing. "In that case maybe I should call her myself."

A shot of panic shook Lily. "What do you mean?" she blurted, her voice trembling. . . .

"I mean, I'll call and find out what she really thinks. Ask her who she suspects is responsible for Graham's death."

"What if—" Lily scarcely dared to breathe. "What if she says she thinks it's you?"

For a long moment Scott didn't answer. When he finally spoke, his voice was just above a whisper. "Then I guess I'll have to set her straight," he said. "I'll have to let her know it was your idea."

"No!" Lily cried in horror. "You can't do that!"

"I *have* to do it," Scott repeated. His voice was so low she had to strain to hear it. "After all, I took a terrible risk, just for you. I did it so you would realize that we're supposed to be together, Lily. If you don't start taking me more seriously, then what choice do I have?"

"But, Scott—"

"We're in this together, Lily. You and me. In it together—forever."

chapter

17

Lily carelessly swept a brush through her hair. She didn't really care how she looked.

I can't believe I'm doing this, she thought.

But what choice did she have? It was Saturday night, and she promised Scott she'd go out with him. Maybe after this date he'd leave her alone for a while.

The hardest part had been getting him to agree to meet her in another part of town so Alex wouldn't find out. Since Alex lived only a block away, there was a good chance he'd see Scott if he picked Lily up at home.

"Night, Dad." Lily stuck her head in the family room before leaving.

"Good night, Lily." He smiled at her. "Going out with Alex?"

"Uh, no," she replied. "Just . . . uh . . . a friend from school."

"Well, have a good time. Glad to see you taking a little time off to have fun."

"Thanks," she murmured.

I'd much rather be studying, she thought as she made her way out the door.

She neared the corner of Old Mill Road when a familiar figure appeared on the sidewalk ahead of her. She felt her heart drop into her shoes.

Alex!

"Lily—hi!" he exclaimed, as surprised as she was.

"Hey, Alex," she replied, trying to cover up her panic.

"You're out? I thought you said you were studying tonight."

"Oh, well . . ." Lily thought fast. "I am. I'm going to the library. I have to look some things up for . . . um . . . for social science."

"I can get Mom's car later. Why don't I pick you up and we can go out for a pizza or something when you're done?"

"I'd like to, Alex," she said. "I really would. Only I promised my dad I'd come right home after I do my research. You know how he is."

"Yeah," Alex grumbled.

Lily reached out and placed a hand on his shoulder. "Thanks anyway."

"Yeah, sure," he said. "Well, talk to you later." He stomped off in the direction of his house.

Lily watched him go for a moment, then sighed. He was angry, she saw. But what could she do about it? Reluctantly she continued on her way.

Scott met her at the bus stop in front of the mall. "You look great," he said cheerfully.

"Thanks," she replied, trying to smile.

"I can't believe we're actually going out," Scott said excitedly. He reached for her hand. His palm felt hot and sweaty.

"What do you want to do?" he asked, pulling her close. "How about a movie and then we'll go for something to eat?"

What an original idea, Lily thought sarcastically.

He suggested a couple of movies playing at the Division Street Sixplex.

"I've seen both of them," she said quickly. "I really want to see that new film with Winona Ryder. You know. The real romantic one."

"Huh?" Scott reacted with surprise. "Where's that playing?"

"In Waynesbridge," she replied. "I'm dying to see it. Please, Scott?"

"Sure," Scott said. "If that's what you really want to see." He opened the door to his father's silver Accord.

Swallowing hard, Lily slid into the car. She had only picked that movie because it was playing in Waynesbridge, twenty miles away. Now no one would see her with Scott.

At the movie theater Scott bought a large bag of

popcorn. Both of them concentrated on eating it. As soon as the bag was empty, Scott grabbed Lily's hand and kept hold of it.

She tried to focus on the film, but all she could think about was Scott, sitting beside her, trying to act like her boyfriend.

I can't stand the touch of his hand, she thought, staring straight ahead. It really gives me the creeps.

Lily pulled her hand away as soon as the closing credits rolled up the screen.

"Great movie," Scott said enthusiastically. "Winona Ryder is really beautiful. She looks like you."

Lily muttered thanks.

"How about Pete's Pizza?" Scott suggested as they walked to the car.

"I'm not really in the mood for pizza," Lily replied.

"Well, then, let's go to the food court. You know. At the Division Street Mall. That way you can have anything you want."

"The mall's too far from here," she said quickly. "I have a better idea. Why don't we go to one of the places in Fort Morris? I've never been there."

Fort Morris was a small town past Waynesbridge. It wasn't the nicest place, but at least they wouldn't bump into anyone from school there.

"Are you serious?" Scott asked. "You want to go to Fort Morris?"

"Why not?" Lily shrugged. "It's an adventure!"

"Yeah. An adventure," Scott agreed.

The main drag in Fort Morris was lined on both

sides with small shopping centers and fast-food places. Lily pointed to a dimly lit restaurant called Burger Buddy. "Let's go there," she urged, pointing.

Scott turned his father's car into the parking lot, which was jammed with low-riders, sports trucks, and motorcycles. A group of tough-looking guys wearing leather sat on the curb, passing around a bottle underneath a neon sign that flashed OOL HALL.

"Are you sure you want to go here?" Scott asked.

"Sure," Lily replied. "Maybe we can play a few games of ool afterward."

He snickered at her joke. But she could see that he was uncomfortable.

She followed him into the crowded, dark restaurant. The booths were packed with young men and women drinking pitchers of beer, and laughing and talking in loud voices. Scott and Lily took a table near the window under a lamp with a missing bulb.

"I can't believe you wanted to come here," Scott said. "This place is a dump."

"I told you, it's an adventure," Lily replied breezily.

The waitress, who had a tattoo of a unicorn on her arm, took their orders, then disappeared into the kitchen.

It was so noisy, Lily felt like holding her hands over her ears. The noise and the strain of being with Scott were beginning to give her a headache. She glanced at her watch, glad to see that it was getting late.

"So I guess you're getting over your shock about

Graham," Scott said, having to shout across the table to be heard.

Lily's jaw dropped open. Her true feelings showed for the first time all night. "How can you say that?"

"Take it easy. I meant that it brought us together— the way we belong."

Lily stared back at him, speechless. He really is crazy, she told herself. Totally insane.

He didn't seem to notice her unhappiness. He smiled at her. "The time's gone really fast tonight, don't you think?"

"Yeah. Fast," Lily said blankly.

Be patient, she instructed herself. The date is almost over. All you have to do is eat. Then you can go home and get away from him.

Lily tuned out while Scott babbled on about the movie. Finally their food arrived. She began to pick at her salad, ignoring him completely.

They were on the way out of the restaurant when the door swung open and three guys walked in.

"Lily!"

At the sound of her name, Lily froze.

"What are you doing here?" the voice called.

Lily stared into Rick's grinning face. "Hello, Rick," she mumbled. She felt her face flush.

The last time she saw Rick, she accused him of making those stupid late-night phone calls. That was before she found out that Scott was making the calls.

But Rick didn't seem the least bit angry.

"Hey, since when do you hang out around here?" he asked, still grinning. He glanced at Scott, sizing him up. "So is this your boyfriend?"

"That's right," Scott replied smugly. He put his arm around Lily's waist and pulled her close.

Rick shrugged. "Hey, take care," he said. He and his friends continued on into the restaurant.

"Who was that?" Scott demanded when they were in the car.

"Someone I work with," Lily told him.

"Oh, yeah?" Scott shot back. "He seemed pretty interested in you."

"He works for my uncle," Lily said. "I hardly know him."

"Well, keep it that way," Scott snapped. "By the way, have you told Alex yet? Have you told him about us?"

"It's still too soon," Lily murmured.

"Now that we're dating," Scott continued, as if he hadn't heard her, "you'll have to tell him."

"I don't want to hurt him," Lily replied. "Give me some time."

Scott sneered at her. "There are no other guys in the picture, Lily. Just me. Get rid of Alex."

Lily didn't answer. Instead she scooted as far as she could on her side of the car.

Scott didn't seem to mind as he chattered on and on about his plans for their future. "After graduation, we can go to college together," he told her. "We'll get married, and maybe move to a big city."

As soon as he pulled up in front of Lily's house, she reached for the door handle.

But he quickly stopped her, drawing her roughly across the seat toward him. "Oh, Lily," he murmured. "Lily." He searched for her lips with his.

Lily's stomach churned. Scott sickened her. She couldn't stand another second with him.

"I have to go in!" she cried shrilly, trying to pull free of his grasp.

"Not yet," he insisted, holding her tighter.

"Scott, my father might be watching!"

Scott glanced through the windshield to the house. There were several lights on on the ground floor. Reluctantly he let her go.

Lily leaped out of the car. Scott hurried over to the passenger side. He took her arm as they walked up the front steps.

"I had a really great time," he told her as they stood together on the porch. "Let's go out again soon."

"Thanks for the movie, Scott," she replied without warmth.

He leaned forward to kiss her. But she quickly pulled open the door and ducked inside. "Good night," she called through the crack before she pulled the door shut. "See you in school."

She stood for a moment with her back against the door, grateful to be home, grateful to be away from Scott, from his mooning eyes, his hot, sweaty hands.

What am I going to do? she asked herself, feeling sick, feeling terrified, feeling helpless.

FINAL GRADE

I can't let him control my life like this.
But how can I ever get rid of him?
There must be some way out, something I can do.
And then she realized there was an answer.
An answer that had been there all along.
I'll kill him, she decided.

chapter
18

On Monday Lily had quizzes in three classes. Luckily, she didn't run into Scott. Then, in last period gym, she remembered it was the day of the regular magazine meeting.

Oh, no, she thought. I've been so busy worrying I'd bump into him in the halls, I must have blotted it out. For a moment she considered ditching the meeting. But Scott would get angry at her, and she didn't want to risk that.

When she got to the magazine office, she was glad to see that no one else had arrived yet. She found a folder in her box containing several stories that Shadyside students had submitted to the magazine. Grateful for something to do, she sat at the editing table and started to read them.

A few minutes later, the office door banged open. Julie came in, followed by Alex.

Julie called out a cheerful greeting. Alex flashed her a quick smile, but didn't say anything.

Lily swallowed hard. Had he somehow heard about her date with Scott?

Julie dumped her books on the table. "I hope this meeting doesn't last long. I've got a million things to do after school."

"So where's Scott?" Alex glanced around. "It's late. Maybe we should start the meeting without him."

Lily started to reply. But Scott came rushing in. "Sorry I'm late." He smiled at Lily. "You look great today," he told her, ignoring the others.

"Thanks," she muttered, keeping her eyes fixed on the papers in front of her.

"Your parents weren't mad the other night—were they?" he continued. "I mean, I didn't want you to get in trouble on our first date."

Lily felt her heart start to pound.

I don't believe it! she thought, shutting her eyes. *I don't believe he's doing this to me in front of everyone.*

Alex had been flipping through a folder of poems. He let it drop to the table as he glanced from Lily to Scott. "What are you talking about?" he demanded.

"He's talking about the editing work we did the other night," Lily said quickly. "We were looking at some stuff for the next issue."

"That's not what I'm talking about," Scott declared.

"Of course it is," Lily insisted in a panic. "Don't you remember?"

"No, Lily. I'm talking about our date." Scott turned to Alex. "Lily and I went out on Saturday night."

"Excuse me?" Alex glared at Lily. "I thought you were studying Saturday night. At the library."

"I can explain," Lily began.

An expression of disgust twisted Alex's face, and he didn't wait for her to finish. Instead he whirled around and stormed out of the room.

"Alex, wait!" Lily ran after him, into the hall. "I can explain—" she repeated.

"Oh, yeah?" Alex spun around to face her. "More lies?"

"It's not what you think!" she insisted.

"Then what is it?" Alex demanded.

She took a deep breath. What could she tell him?

What?

Definitely not the truth—that Scott was a murderer who was controlling her every move.

"Well?" Alex snapped. "I'm waiting."

When she didn't speak up, he started backing down the hall. "I don't get it, Lily. I thought you and I were a couple. So why did you go out with Scott?"

"Alex, please—" Lily pleaded.

"And I'll tell you something else!" he shouted. "I'm sick and tired of having to put up with your moods lately. And your studying like a crazy person all the time."

"It's going to change," she said feebly. "I know I don't spend a lot of time with you. But—"

"Forget it!" Alex cut her off. "I don't want to hear it. Have fun with Scott!"

"But I'm not interested in Scott!" she cried. "Please believe me."

She reached out for his hand. But he shook her away as if she were a bug that had somehow crawled onto his fingers.

Then, without another word, he stalked off down the hall.

Lily stood watching him until he disappeared around the corner. She wrapped her arms tightly around herself, as if trying to hold herself together.

It's over, she realized. Because of Scott, I've lost Alex forever.

The next few days, whenever Lily saw Alex in the halls at school, he stared at her as if she were invisible.

She forced herself to concentrate on school and her job so she wouldn't have to think about how much she missed him. Luckily, the end of the semester was almost here, and the teachers began piling on the homework. Lily had plenty to keep her busy.

One night while she was working at her uncle's store, the phone rang. "Bob's Drugstore," Lily said into the handset. "May I help you?"

"Lily? It's Julie."

"Julie? Hi."

"Sorry to call you at work," Julie said breathlessly. "But I've got to tell you what I found out. You know how I've been trying to find out more about how Graham died?"

Lily felt a cold shiver run down her back. "Yes?"

"Well, I think I know who murdered Graham!"

chapter

19

"You what?" Lily could hardly speak.

"I spoke to the night foreman at the plant," Julie continued. "He told me he discovered a message for Graham. On the answering machine at the printing plant. It was left the night he died. The police didn't think it was important because they're convinced Graham's death was an accident. But from what Mr. Jacobson said—I think I know who left the message!"

Lily's heart thudded in her chest. She squeezed the phone so hard, her hand ached. "Who . . . who do you think left the message?"

"I can't tell you for sure till I hear the tape," Julie explained. "The plant is closed tonight, but I'm going over there tomorrow. And then—maybe I'll have enough information to go to the police."

Lily listened to her friend with mounting horror. The message had to be from Scott.

"Lily? Are you still there?" Julie demanded.

Lily didn't answer for a moment. She was desperately trying to think of something to make Julie back off.

"Anyone could have left a message for Graham," Lily told her friend. "It doesn't mean that person killed him."

"It may not be complete proof," Julie agreed. "But it's definitely an important clue—enough to make the police open the case. Besides, Mr. Jacobson, the foreman, doesn't think Graham's death was an accident, either."

"Why not?" Lily's heart beat faster and faster.

"He said he's never seen anyone fall into the press the way Graham did. He said you'd almost *have* to be pushed!" Julie explained. "So I think—"

The bell above the pharmacy door jangled.

"A customer just came in," Lily interrupted. "Can I call you back?"

"Sure," Julie replied. "But my mom's been waiting to use the phone. The line may be busy."

"Okay. I'll try to call you back in a couple of minutes." Lily hung up and forced herself to smile. "May I help you?" she said to the customer, an elderly man using a cane.

"I came to pick up my prescription," he said. He walked slowly up to the counter. "The name is Lightner." Lily turned to the bin of prescriptions on the back shelf and began shuffling through the envelopes in the *L* section.

"I'm sorry," she said. "I don't have a prescription here. I'll have to check in the back." She glanced at her watch, then crossed to the back room where her uncle was working.

"Lightner?" her uncle said. "Oh, yes, I have it here." He pointed to a pile of prescriptions on the wide counter where he worked. Slowly he rummaged through the stack.

Lily waited anxiously, trying her best not to look impatient. She had to find out what else Julie knew.

Julie thought she knew who the murderer was. Did she suspect Scott? Did she suspect him even before hearing the tape?

"Lily?"

Her uncle held the prescription envelope out to her.

"Sorry," she said. "I was thinking about . . . about my homework."

"You work too hard." He smiled warmly at her, then turned back to the prescriptions.

Lily hurried back out front and rang up Mr. Lightner's prescription while the old man slowly fingered through his wallet for his money.

Finally he left, and Lily picked up the phone. But before she could call Julie back, two teenage girls came in and hurried to the makeup display. They spent about fifteen minutes examining different kinds of mascara and asking Lily about them.

Please leave! Lily urged silently. *Please! I've got an important call to make!*

At last the girls bought their cosmetics and made their way out. Lily punched in Julie's number as Rick swaggered over to the counter. "What's up? How's it going with your boyfriend?"

"Fine." She hung up the phone. Then she frowned at him and sighed with impatience.

"I was really surprised to meet him the other night," Rick continued, not taking a hint. "Somehow he didn't look like the kind of guy I picture you with."

"Rick, please, I have a lot to do."

"Okay, okay." Rick held up his hands. "I won't bug you. Besides, I promised your uncle I'd help him reinforce some shelves in the back." He disappeared through the door into the back room.

Lily turned back to the phone.

But the bell over the door rang again. "I don't believe this!" she exclaimed. She glanced toward the door and saw Scott approaching her, a yellow rose in his hand.

He smiled. "This is for you." He held out the rose.

"Oh, Scott," she said in exasperation, ignoring the flower. "It's almost closing time. I've got a million things to do."

His smile melted. "You're not being very friendly. I came all the way across town to see you." He placed the flower down and leaned toward her. "You must be really tired. That's why you sound so stressed out."

Lily backed away. "I'm not tired—I'm working."

"So what?" Scott said. "That shouldn't make any difference. Don't you get it yet, Lily? Whatever you're doing—we're together."

"Scott, I have to—"

"It doesn't matter!" he snapped. He took both her hands in his and pulled her across the counter till their faces were an inch apart. "I think about you all the time," he said. "Tell me you think about me too."

She hesitated. His grip on her hands tightened. She thought about screaming, then changed her mind.

Rick was hammering in the back room, and she'd have to yell loudly. Besides, who knew how Scott would react if she screamed?

"Give me a kiss," he demanded.

"No. Scott. Please—"

"One kiss, Lily!" His voice grew angrier, more insistent.

She closed her eyes and forced her lips to brush his.

Scott grabbed her tighter, pulling her over the counter.

"Let me go!" she cried. She wrenched away from him and backed up against the shelves.

Scott stared at her, breathing hard, his expression one of surprise. "Lily, that wasn't much of a kiss. What's your problem? Don't you even want the rose?"

She shook her head.

Scott's eyes narrowed. "You can't ever get away from me," he warned, lowering his voice to sound menacing. "Not at work, not anywhere. Don't you know that yet? It's you and me forever, Lily. Got it?"

Something inside Lily snapped. I can't take his threats any longer! she realized.

"It's not forever!" she shrieked, the words bursting

from her. "It's not forever, Scott. In fact, it's all going to come to an end—real soon!"

"What are you talking about?" Scott demanded.

"I'm talking about Julie," Lily breathlessly blurted out.

"Huh? Julie? What about Julie?"

"She's figuring out the truth, Scott!" Lily told him, spitting out the words, her chest heaving, her heart pounding.

"You're lying!" he cried.

"No, I'm not," Lily replied. "She found out that someone left a message at the printing plant for Graham the night he was killed. It was you, wasn't it? You left that message, didn't you, Scott?"

For a moment Scott didn't answer. "What if I did?" he snarled. "It was harmless enough."

"The foreman doesn't think so. Neither does Julie. What did you say?"

Scott turned away for a moment, thinking. "I asked Graham to meet me at the plant. I told him it was about the magazine." He shrugged. "No problem. I'll destroy the message tape."

"Too late!" Lily cried. "The foreman knows about the message, and Julie is very close to the truth. It won't be long before she tells the police!"

"How do you know all this?"

"She just called me. She told me."

Lily stared at him, waiting to hear him panic.

But when he spoke his voice came out calm and cold. "Well, I'm sorry about that."

"What do you mean?"

"I mean, I'm sorry for Julie," Scott said softly. "I can't let her go to the police."

"You can't stop her, Scott."

"Yes, I can," he replied. "If Julie tells the police what she knows, she'll ruin two lives, Lily—yours and mine. We can't let that happen, can we?"

Lily gasped. "You mean—?"

"That's right," Scott declared. "We have to kill her."

chapter

20

*L*ily buried her face in her hands. *He's crazy,* she told herself. *He's sick. And he's dangerous.*

Everything is out of control. How could I let this go so far? I lost control.

But I can't afford to lose control.

Got to think. Got to think.

What am I going to do now?

Lily took a deep breath, forcing herself to calm down. You've got to pretend to be on his side, she instructed herself. At least until you can think of a way out.

She dropped her hands to her sides and faced him. "Maybe we can talk her out of it, Scott. We can make her think she's wrong, that she made a mistake—"

"It won't work," he said. "If she really suspects that I killed Graham, she won't give up, Lily."

"I can change her mind," Lily pleaded. "Scott, she's my best friend—"

"I know she's your best friend. That's too bad," Scott said. "But she has to die. You understand, right? You know we have no choice."

"Lily?" Uncle Bob stepped out from the back room.

She sighed with relief. Maybe she could keep her uncle here, keep him talking, until Scott left. And then she'd be able to figure out what to do.

"Hello, Scott." Uncle Bob smiled as he recognized Scott. "How's your mother doing?" Scott's mother and Uncle Bob's wife were good friends.

"She's fine," Scott answered politely.

"Glad to hear it," responded Uncle Bob. He turned to Lily. "You can go home now," he told her. "I'm going to lock up."

"But it's still early," Lily protested.

"Not that early," he said, glancing at his watch. "Besides, Rick and I are going to be busy for a while rebuilding the shelves in the back."

"Is there anything else I can help you with?" Lily asked, eager to stay, desperate to get rid of Scott.

"You sound as if you don't *want* to have a little extra time off," Uncle Bob said with a smile. "You work too hard, Lily. Enjoy yourself for a change. Go out for a soda with Scott."

"That's a great idea," Scott said, grinning.

"But—I need to alphabetize the prescriptions for tomorrow," Lily insisted.

"Nonsense," Uncle Bob replied. "Rick and I have everything under control. You have a nice evening." He disappeared again into the back of the store. Lily could hear the loud hammering start up again.

As soon as Uncle Bob was out of earshot, Scott turned to her, his eyes gleaming. "I want you to call Julie and tell her to meet you at the printing plant."

"The printing plant? Why?" Lily demanded.

"This time you're going to help me, Lily. I've committed murder for you. Now it's your turn to help me."

"I—I won't help you, Scott," Lily stammered.

"Oh, yes, you will. You don't have a choice." He motioned to the phone. "Now call her and tell her to meet you at the plant."

"Why would she agree to go there?" Lily asked. "We already printed the magazine."

"Tell her you called Mr. Jacobson. Say that he agreed to let you in tonight. Julie wants to hear the message tape, doesn't she?"

"Yes, but—"

"Just *do* it."

Lily stared back at him but didn't move. I won't do it, she thought. I won't lure my best friend to her death.

"I said *do* it!" Scott repeated. He grabbed Lily's wrist and began to squeeze. "Call her, Lily, call her now."

"No!" Lily cried. "No, I won't! I won't!"

Gripping Lily's wrist with one hand, Scott jerked

the phone from the back of the counter. He began to punch in Julie's number.

"You'll call her now," he growled. "You'll do exactly what I say!"

Lily tried to pull her hand away, but Scott's grip was too strong.

"It's ringing," Scott told her. He let go of her hand. "Now talk to her!"

Instead, Lily slammed the phone onto its cradle.

Scott's face darkened. He edged around the counter, breathing hard. He brought his face close to hers, his eyes blazing furiously. "You'll do as I say, Lily," he said softly. "You don't really have a choice."

Desperately, Lily pulled open the small drawer where her uncle kept his gun. If she could reach it in time . . .

With an angry cry Scott clamped his hand over her wrist.

Then he reached into the drawer and grabbed the pistol.

With a quick, hard motion he shoved the gun barrel into Lily's chest.

"Now call her!" he snarled.

chapter
21

As she rode with Scott toward the printing plant, Lily searched her mind for a way out. But nothing came to her. She gazed out the window at the black night.

If only a police car would come by, she thought. But the road was almost completely deserted.

When Lily called Julie from her uncle's pharmacy, Julie had sounded so excited to hear Lily's voice. "Wait till you hear what else I've found out, Lil!" she exclaimed.

"Great," Lily murmured without enthusiasm.

Then Scott pressed the barrel of the gun against her head, and she did what he wanted. "I called Mr. Jacobson," she lied to Julie. "He says he'll let us in if we go to the plant right away."

"Oh, wow!" Julie reacted excitedly. She was eager to hear the message tape. "It won't take me long. I'll meet you there, Lil."

Now Lily and Scott were speeding through the night, hurrying to the printing plant to meet Julie. "You did fine, Lily," Scott said, interrupting her thoughts. "Just fine."

"What?" Lily turned away from the window and glanced at Scott, hunched over the steering wheel.

"I said you did fine," he repeated. "When you talked to Julie. I'm sure she doesn't suspect a thing."

"Scott, please let me just talk to her," Lily begged again. "I'll convince her that Graham died by accident. I'm sure I can do it."

"I already told you no," Scott snapped impatiently. "I already told you that there's only one thing we can do. You're not listening to me, Lily."

"Yes, I am, I just—"

"We're going to kill her. What else can we do?"

Lily remained silent for the rest of the ride. They turned into the parking lot, and she stepped out of the car. She glanced around the dark lot, thinking for a moment that she might try to run.

But then Julie will be alone, she realized. I can't abandon her.

The front door to the printing plant was locked. But Scott still had his key. He opened the door, then slipped inside, leaving the door slightly ajar. Inside the plant, it was as dark as a tomb.

"Come on," Scott urged, pushing the gun into Lily's ribs. "Let's go in the back."

"Scott, please don't do this," she pleaded in a trembling whisper.

"This way," he replied roughly.

Dim lights glowed against the wall in the huge press room. When Lily saw the bulky silhouette of the press, she shuddered and looked away.

Once again she saw Graham there, wedged into the giant paper cylinder, crushed and broken.

Scott grabbed Lily's elbow and drew her into a small area between the wall and the huge machine. "We'll hide here. Julie will walk right into our trap."

"We'll never get away with it," Lily warned him. "Nobody will ever believe that someone else had an accident here."

"Don't worry," Scott said. "I'm going to set this one up differently. It's going to look as if Julie surprised an intruder—and that the intruder shot her."

"Scott, please, no—" Lily begged.

"I'll throw the gun somewhere in the Fear Street Woods," Scott continued, his eyes glowing excitedly in the dim light. "Nobody will ever find it."

"I . . . I don't care what happens to me," Lily began desperately. "I don't care if I go to jail. Anything is better than letting you kill Julie."

Scott snickered, a dry, cold laugh. "You say that now," he said. "But you wouldn't say that if the police actually suspected you. Come on, Lily, stop acting so innocent. You know you wanted me to kill Graham."

"No! No, I didn't—"

"You wanted him dead, Lily! Admit it. All you cared about was being valedictorian!"

"No, Scott! You're wrong!"

"Now we've got to kill Julie to stay safe. To stay together. It won't be hard, Lily. You'll see."

She started to protest. But what was the point? She knew he wasn't listening to anything she said. She knew that no matter what she did, he was going to kill Julie, to shoot her when she entered the room.

As Lily huddled in the dark next to Scott, she thought back over the past few months. She'd been totally obsessed with her grades, with beating Graham for valedictorian. Now it all seemed so silly, even meaningless. Lily had paid a terrible price for her dream—Graham was dead, and she'd lost Alex, as well.

I can't let my best friend die too, Lily thought. I can't let Scott hurt her.

After what seemed like hours, she heard the sound of a car pulling into the gravel lot outside.

"She's here!" Scott whispered.

A car door slammed. A few seconds later Lily heard a creaking noise as the front door opened.

"Lily?" came a faint voice. "Lily? Is anyone here? Lily? Hello?"

An icy chill passed through Lily as her best friend stepped into the room.

Beside her, Scott raised the pistol.

chapter

22

"Lily?" Julie called. "Lily, are you in here?"

Lily watched Julie step uncertainly through the doorway to the reception area. She took several steps toward the printing press, her sneakers scuffing on the concrete floor.

Lily took a deep breath. Then screamed at the top of her lungs: *"Run, Julie! Run!"*

Pushing off from the wall, Lily ducked away from Scott. Then she dived around to the side of the press.

"Julie—watch out! Run!"

But Julie didn't move from where she stood.

"What's going on?" she called in confusion. "Lily, where are you?"

Bending low as he ran, Scott plunged into the

middle of the room. He aimed the pistol at Julie. "Stop right there!" he commanded.

Julie gasped. Her mouth dropped open in shock. "Scott? Is that you?"

He didn't reply. He trained the gun on Julie's chest.

"What's going on?" Julie cried. Even in the dim light Lily could see the fear grow in her eyes. "What are you doing with that gun? Where's Lily?"

"I'm here!" Lily cried from her crouched position beside the printing press. "I tried to warn you, Julie. I tried—"

"Warn me about what?" Julie cried shrilly. "You asked me to meet you here. To hear the tape . . . the tape about . . ." Her voice trailed off as she put together the pieces. "About Graham's death," she finished softly.

"That's right," Scott said. "What *about* Graham's death, Julie?"

"Scott? It was you?" Julie asked in a trembling voice that barely carried across the room. "You?"

"That's right," Scott said.

Julie uttered a hoarse cry of surprise. "I thought I was so close to figuring it out. But I guess I wasn't. I *never* dreamed it was you."

"You're not exactly Nancy Drew—are you?" Scott replied scornfully. "Too bad anyway."

"What . . ." Julie's voice wavered. "What do you mean?"

"I don't have a choice," Scott replied, waving the pistol. "I really can't let you leave here—can I?"

"I won't tell anyone!" Julie shrieked. "I'll keep this—"

Scott shook his head. "Sorry, Julie. I really am."

"Lily?" Julie's voice was pleading, shaking with terror. "Lily—tell Scott I can keep a secret. Tell him. *Do* something."

Lily stood up. "He—he won't listen to me," she stammered.

She began to edge toward Scott.

He swung the gun in her direction. "Where are you going?"

Lily stopped short. He would kill her in a flash. She had no doubt about that.

Scott turned the gun back to Julie. "Lily helped murder Graham. Did you know that?"

"Huh?" Julie gasped.

"I did not!" Lily shrieked.

Scott ignored her. "She wanted Graham to die. I did it all for her. Lily knew everything right from the beginning."

Julie turned, horrified, to Lily. "Is that true? Please tell me it isn't true!"

"It isn't true!" Lily cried. "I didn't know Scott did it till after the funeral. I never wanted him to. I never asked him to kill Graham. Julie—you've *got* to believe me!"

Julie pressed her hands against the sides of her face. Her eyes were wide with horror. "I don't know *what* to believe!" she cried. "I always thought you were my best friend—"

"I *am* your best friend," Lily insisted. "And I

always will be. Scott, I'm begging you! Let Julie go. Please!"

He shook his head. "We're wasting time with all this talk. Julie, come here."

"No." Her hands still pressed against her face, she began to back toward the reception area.

"I said, come here!" Scott shouted angrily.

"No!" Julie turned and started to run.

Scott bolted after her. With an angry cry he grabbed her arm. Wrenched her around. Began to drag her toward the press.

"No! Scott, no! Let me go! Please don't hurt me!" Julie wailed.

"This way!" Scott shoved her hard against the press.

Julie slumped against the big machine, trembling in fright.

Breathing hard, making shrill wheezing noises, Scott raised the gun.

He stood less than a foot from Julie.

There's no way he'll miss, Lily realized.

"No," Julie pleaded. "No, no, no!"

Taking a deep breath, Lily hurled herself at Scott.

She slapped wildly at the hand gripping the pistol.

"Let her go!" Lily shrieked. She grabbed Scott's wrist. Struggled to pull the pistol away.

"Stop it!" Scott shouted. He tried to wrench away, but Lily tightened her grip, forcing down his arm.

"Get out of here, Julie! Go!" Lily shouted.

With a powerful tug Scott yanked his hand free.

"I won't let you do it!" Lily cried.

She threw herself again at Scott.

With a groan he raised his arm high, then brought the butt of the pistol down hard on her shoulder.

Lily uttered a cry of pain. She fell against the side of the printing press.

As she struggled to gain her balance, she saw Scott turn back to Julie.

But Julie had vanished.

Scott let out a furious cry. "Where are you, Julie?" Frantically he began running one direction, then the other, searching for her.

She got away, Lily thought, breathing a little easier. She rubbed her aching shoulder. Julie got away.

But a scraping sound from behind the press made Lily's heart sink. Lily realized that Julie hadn't escaped after all. She was hiding in the nook between the press and the wall.

Scott spun toward the back wall. "I know you're back there, Julie!"

"Julie, stay quiet!" Lily instructed.

Too late. Scott stepped around the press and found Julie crouched in the corner.

Lily heard a metallic click. Scott had cocked the gun.

She pulled herself to her feet. Maybe she could stop him.

She heard Julie scream. "Scott, no!"

Then she heard a loud *crack* as the gun fired.

chapter

23

The room tilted and swayed. The floor seemed to rise up in front of her as Lily dived behind the press to get to Julie.

Too late.

Too late. Too late.

Julie lay sprawled awkwardly on her back on the floor, her head tilted up against the wall, one leg bent beneath her.

"It's over," Scott said, almost calmly. "She won't bother us anymore." He stood staring down at Julie's body, his face a blank, the gun gripped at his side.

Lily crouched next to her friend's lifeless form. Never again would she see Julie's smile or hear her voice. Never again would the two of them hang out at school or at the mall or at one another's houses.

"Oh, Julie," Lily sobbed. "I'm sorry. I'm so, so sorry."

Lily's breaths came in convulsive gasps. Her best friend lay dead in front of her. And it was all her fault.

"Forget about Julie," Scott said softly. "We've got to cover this up and get out of here."

"Who cares?" Lily sobbed. "How could you do this, Scott? How could you kill her too?"

"You knew there was no choice," Scott replied. "Now we've got to make sure we don't leave any evidence. You find the answering machine and get the tape. I'll wipe off everything we touched so they won't find our fingerprints."

Lily didn't move. She wasn't sure she *could* move.

Scott shoved the pistol into his jeans pocket. He leaned over Lily. "Hurry. Get up. Help me clean things up."

"No!" she cried. "No!" She struggled to crawl away from him. "You killed her!" she sobbed. "You killed my best friend."

"I did it for both of us! Don't you understand that?"

"No!" Lily screamed. She flailed against him.

Pulled the pistol out of his pocket.

"Give me that!" Scott made a desperate grab for it. Missed.

Lily struggled to steady the gun firmly in both hands.

"Give it! Give!" Scott reached out a hand for it.

She shook her head. "No, Scott. It's over now."

"Take it easy, Lily." Scott backed up against the wall behind the press. "Let me have the gun back, Lily. You're upset. You don't know what you're doing."

"I know exactly what I'm doing," Lily replied coldly. Her eyes fell on a wall phone hanging behind the press. "I want you to pick up that phone, Scott. I want you to dial the police."

Scott's eyes bulged in disbelief. "The police?" he said. "Are you crazy?"

"Not now," Lily replied. "I was crazy before, when I let you get away with killing Graham."

"Do you know what will happen if I call the police?" Scott demanded. "They won't just come after me, Lily. They'll come after you too. I'll tell them you were in on Graham's death. And I'll tell them it was your idea to kill Julie!"

He took a step toward Lily. "Your fingerprints are on the gun now. Only your fingerprints."

"I don't care!" she cried. "Pick up the phone! Pick it up now!"

"They'll never believe you," Scott insisted. "Why don't you come to your senses? You're in this as deep as I am!"

"Call them!" Lily repeated, stabbing the air with the pistol.

"Lily—"

Lily gripped the gun even tighter. Her hands shook violently, but her aim didn't waver. "Do it, Scott," she ordered. "Do it now or I'll shoot."

Scott didn't move. He stared back at her, frozen, not blinking. And then, to Lily's surprise, he started to laugh.

"Call them!" Lily commanded again. "Pick up the phone and call the police!"

"I'm not afraid of you." Scott snickered. "You could never kill me!"

"Yes I could!" Lily replied heatedly. "And I will— unless you do what I say."

"You'll never hurt me, Lily. Never." He took a step toward her.

"Get back!" she shouted. "I'm serious, Scott! Get back or I'll shoot!"

"No. No way." He took another step forward.

Lily willed herself to pull the trigger, to squeeze down on it, to shoot Scott.

But her finger wouldn't respond.

He was right. She couldn't do it.

She let out a cry as he leaped forward and grabbed the gun away.

He laughed, pleased with himself. She drew back. But he wrapped both arms around her. Pulled her close to him. Held her tight, too tight to break away.

"It's you and me," he whispered into her hair.

Lily's knees buckled as he held her tight. She felt sick.

Why didn't I shoot him? Why couldn't I pull the trigger?

A rustling noise from the floor startled her.

Lily turned toward the wall—and froze in horror.

Uncurling slowly, her eyes half open, her mouth twisted in pain, Julie's corpse was climbing up from the floor.

chapter
_____
24

 L ily watched in silent shock as the corpse pulled itself up.

Julie's eyes stared blankly ahead. She staggered forward, raising her arms like those of a sleepwalker.

"We've got a lot to do now," Scott was saying. He had his back to the walking corpse. He didn't read the look of shock on Lily's face.

Lily watched Julie pick up a heavy metal bar from on top of the press.

Moving faster now, moving steadier, the corpse stepped up behind Scott.

Raised the metal bar.

And brought it down heavily on the back of Scott's head.

The bar hit with a loud *crack*.

Scott didn't react at all for a second or two.

Then a choked gurgle escaped his open mouth. His eyes rolled up in his head. His knees bent, and he crumpled to the concrete floor.

Lily hadn't moved. She hadn't made a sound.

Finally she found her voice. "Julie—you're—you're—dead!"

"No. I'm okay, Lily," Julie replied. "I'm okay."

"Scott shot you! I saw him!" Lily insisted.

"He didn't shoot me!" Julie said. "He didn't hurt me at all."

Lily let out a joyful cry. She leaped forward, stepped around Scott's crumpled body, and wrapped Julie in a long, emotional hug.

"You're okay . . . okay . . ." Lily kept repeating.

Finally they broke apart. "What happened?" Lily demanded. "How—?"

"I don't know," Julie replied, shaking her head. "I don't know what happened. Maybe the gun misfired. When it went off, I fell to the floor. I was so terrified. I must have hit my head and passed out. But when I came to, I realized I wasn't hurt."

"But you didn't even move!" Lily cried. "I thought for sure you were dead."

"That's what I wanted Scott to think."

"So you heard everything we said?"

"Yes," Julie nodded. "I can't believe Scott killed Graham—I can't believe how crazy he is."

"Julie, I'm so sorry about everything. . . ."

Julie held up a hand to silence her. "It's over now," she said softly. She glanced down at Scott's body.

"We'd better call the police. And an ambulance. Scott needs help—fast."

Lily dropped to her knees as her friend hurried to the phone. She suddenly felt weary, so weary she could barely move.

It's finally over, she told herself. Scott can't hurt me or anyone else anymore.

Julie hung up the phone and sat down beside Lily. Then, together in the dark, empty printing plant, the two friends waited, listening for the wail of sirens.

"Do you hear anything?" Julie asked softly, gazing to the door across the vast room.

"Not yet," Lily replied. "But I think—OHHH!"

She uttered a terrified cry as a hand grabbed her leg.

chapter
25

*L*ily jumped to her feet.

Scott's hand slid weakly off her leg.

On his stomach on the floor, he had crawled over to her, leaving a dark trail of blood behind him. He raised his head with a groan.

His hair was matted by clots of blood. Rivulets of blood poured down his face. "You . . . and . . . me . . . Lily," he spluttered. Blood gushed from his mouth as he struggled to speak. "You . . . and . . . me . . ."

Lily and Julie drew back in revulsion.

Scott raised his hand, making one last feeble grab for Lily's leg. Then he sank facedown into his own puddling blood and was still.

The police and medic squad arrived ten seconds later.

"I can't believe it's over," Lily murmured as she and Julie stepped out into the cool night air.

"Believe it," said Julie. "It is. Scott will never bother you again."

It was nearly midnight, and the police had finally finished questioning the girls. Lily and Julie stood on the sidewalk watching as the police cars disappeared down the street.

Lily yawned. "I'm so tired all I want to do is sleep for about a month."

"Me, too," Julie agreed. "But believe it or not, it's back to the real world. School tomorrow." She unlocked the passenger side of her mother's Corolla for Lily.

"Dad called," Lily told her. "He can't leave Mom. He sounded so happy that we were okay. He actually started to cry. My big, macho dad. Do you believe it?"

Before Julie could reply, another car drove up, stopping beside the Corolla.

"Uncle Bob!" Lily cried in surprise.

Both doors on the other car opened. Uncle Bob and Rick piled out.

"Are you girls all right?" Uncle Bob asked anxiously, peering into the car.

"Everything's okay now," Lily told him.

"Your father phoned me as soon as he heard from the police," Uncle Bob said. "Rick and I were still working. We hurried right over—"

"Thanks a lot, but it's all over," Lily said, sighing. "We're both okay."

"Well, come on, Rick. Guess we're too late to be helpful," Uncle Bob said, scratching his balding head. He peered in at the two girls. "Do you feel all right about driving home alone?"

"Yeah. We can make it okay," Lily replied.

"By the way, Lily," Uncle Bob said, leaning into the car. "I don't suppose you know what happened to the starter pistol I keep in the drawer under the cash register?"

Lily's mouth dropped open. "Huh? Starter pistol? You mean—"

Uncle Bob chuckled. "Did you think that thing was *real?* I wouldn't keep a real gun around. Too scary."

Lily and Julie both burst out laughing.

"Well, that explains a lot!" Lily cried happily. "It explains why Julie is still alive."

They all said good night. A short while later Julie headed her car toward Lily's house.

"That guy Rick is kind of cute," Julie said, glancing at Lily. "He works with you?"

Lily nodded.

"Does he have a girlfriend?"

"Oh, I don't believe it!" Lily cried. "How can you think about boys now after—after—"

"Does he have a girlfriend or not?" Julie persisted.

"No," Lily told her. Then they both burst out laughing.

"Well, it's been a horrible nightmare," Julie said,

pulling the car up Lily's driveway. "I guess you learned one important thing, huh?"

"Huh? What's that?" Lily demanded.

"That there are more important things than being valedictorian."

"No way!" Lily exclaimed. "We've still got four more weeks of school. I'm going to finish first, Julie. I *know* I am!"

About the Author

"Where do you get your ideas?"

That's the question that R. L. Stine is asked most often. "I don't know where my ideas come from," he says. "But I do know that I have a lot more scary stories in my mind that I can't wait to write."

So far, he has written over fifty mysteries and thrillers for young people, all of them bestsellers.

Bob grew up in Columbus, Ohio. Today he lives in an apartment near Central Park in New York City with his wife, Jane, and fourteen-year-old son, Matt.

THE NIGHTMARES
NEVER END . . .
WHEN YOU VISIT

Next: *SWITCHED*
(Coming in May)

When Nicole Darwin's best friend, Lucy Kramer, suggests "Let's switch bodies," Nicole thinks she's joking. But Lucy is serious. She has learned the secret of the mysterious wall that lies deep in the Fear Street woods, just beyond the old Simon mansion. It's called the Changing Wall and, long ago, people called upon its magic to switch bodies.

Nicole thinks, why not make the switch? When we get tired of being each other, we'll return to the woods and switch again.

But what happens when one girl disappears forever? Is there no turning back?

R.L. Stine

- [ ] *THE NEW GIRL*.................74649-9/$3.99
- [ ] *THE SURPRISE PARTY*....73561-6/$3.99
- [ ] *THE OVERNIGHT*.............74650-2/$3.99
- [ ] *MISSING*..........................69410-3/$3.99
- [ ] *THE WRONG NUMBER*.....69411-1/$3.99
- [ ] *THE SLEEPWALKER*........74652-9/$3.99
- [ ] *HAUNTED*.........................74651-0/$3.99
- [ ] *HALLOWEEN PARTY*........70243-2/$3.99
- [ ] *THE STEPSISTER*.............70244-0/$3.99
- [ ] *SKI WEEKEND*..................72480-0/$3.99
- [ ] *THE FIRE GAME*...............72481-9/$3.99
- [ ] *THE THRILL CLUB*............78581-8/$3.99
- [ ] *LIGHTS OUT*....................72482-7/$3.99
- [ ] *TRUTH or DARE*................86836-5/$3.99

- [ ] *THE SECRET BEDROOM*.....72483-5/$3.99
- [ ] *THE KNIFE*........................72484-3/$3.99
- [ ] *THE PROM QUEEN*.............72485-1/$3.99
- [ ] *FIRST DATE*......................73865-8/$3.99
- [ ] *THE BEST FRIEND*.............73866-6/$3.99
- [ ] *THE CHEATER*...................73867-4/$3.99
- [ ] *SUNBURN*.........................73868-2/$3.99
- [ ] *THE NEW BOY*...................73869-0/$3.99
- [ ] *THE DARE*.........................73870-4/$3.99
- [ ] *BAD DREAMS*....................78569-9/$3.99
- [ ] *DOUBLE DATE*...................78570-2/$3.99
- [ ] *ONE EVIL SUMMER*............78596-6/$3.99
- [ ] *THE MIND READER*.............78600-8/$3.99
- [ ] *WRONG NUMBER 2*............78607-5/$3.99
- [ ] *DEAD END*........................86837-3/$3.99
- [ ] *FINAL GRADE*....................86838-1/$3.99
- [ ] *SWITCHED*........................86839-X/$3.99
- [ ] *COLLEGE WEEKEND*....86840-3/$3.99

SUPER CHILLER

- [ ] *PARTY SUMMER*......72920-9/$3.99
- [ ] *BROKEN HEARTS*.....78609-1/$3.99
- [ ] *THE DEAD LIFEGUARD* ....86834-9/$3.99
- [ ] *BAD MOONLIGHT* ....89424-2/$3.99

When the cheers turn to screams...

FEAR STREET®

CHEERLEADERS

The First Evil
75117-4/$3.99

The Second Evil
75118-2/$3.99

The Third Evil
75119-0/$3.99

Available from Archway Paperbacks
Published by Pocket Books